Reasons She Goes to the Woods

Deborah Kay Davies

Reasons She Goes to the Woods

Deborah Kay Davies

ONEWORLD

A Oneworld Book

First published in North America, Great Britain & Australia
by Oneworld Publications, 2014

Copyright © Deborah Kay Davies 2014

The moral right of Deborah Kay Davies to be identified as the
Author of this work has been asserted by her in accordance
with the Copyright, Designs, and Patents Act 1988

ISBN 978-1-78074-376-9
ISBN 978-1-78074-377-6 (eBook)

Typeset by Tetragon, London
Printed and bound by
CPI Group (UK) Ltd, Croydon, CR0 4YY

This is a work of fiction. While, as in all fiction, the literary
perceptions and insights are based on experience, all names,
characters, places, and incidents either are products of
the author's imagination or are used fictitiously.

Oneworld Publications
10 Bloomsbury Street
London WC1B 3SR
England

As always,
for Norman,
with love.

Pearl and her Father

Pearl is perched astride her father's knee. Rain taps the front window and she can just make out, all along the wavering hedge, wet purple flowers that look just like miniature bunches of grapes. Here in the lounge the lamplight reaches out to rest on the carpet ridges and the stiff pleats bordering the cushions. She and her father are in a hideaway; he sits on the yellow-and-navy settee and she sits on him. It's wonderful. But it makes her stomach growl, every time she's with him. She plays with his sleep-soft hands, placing them on her cheeks. When she lets go, they flop back onto his lap, and she lifts them again. His lips are parted and she can see a wink of teeth. His eyes are closed, his breathing rhythmic and deep. She brings her face up close so that the room is filled with her father's regular, heartbreaking features. Her small, strong hands are pressed to his chest. She rests her forehead on his, wanting to get inside. She inhales the smell of his neck deeply and squirms a little; his knee between her legs feels solid and warm. The living room is quiet. In the entire world there is only Pearl and her father. Her mother laid a fire before she went out; taking ages, leaving instructions, dropping things, then slamming the door and coming back. Now Pearl listens to the sounds coming from the grate as the flames lick each other and purr. From the place pressed against her father's knee she feels a rippling sensation move through her body, as if a delicate, frilled mushroom were expanding, elongating, filling her up. She exhales slowly. She mustn't disturb him. He would push her off with his beautiful hands if he woke up.

Pram

Pearl is playing with worms in the front garden. Just where the earth is semi-solid and often splashed with rainwater is the perfect place for them. Pearl loves the wriggly, neat casts they leave behind. Especially she loves the way the worms clump together and make themselves into glistening, slow-moving balls. She gets lost in the task of unknotting them. When they are freed, the worms are usually kinky, and she works each one between her palms until it relaxes. Then she lays them out on the smooth mud. Today, in the middle of the lawn there is a huge black pram. Pearl has ignored the snuffling sounds coming from under the white blanket, and the tasselled corner that droops enticingly over the pram's lacquered side. Her worms are neatly arranged in rows. Now she is drawn to the pram with its moving cover. The hood is up and the inside seems filled with light. She can see a tiny patch of pink cheek and a scribble of hair. She leans in and inhales the smell of baby flesh and warm plastic. Suddenly she feels huge and dirty, her knees and hands caked with mud. Pearl climbs up onto a wheel and pushes herself in beside the baby. Her legs are too long so she bends them to fit. Her head is crushed inside the hood. She breathes quietly, and with her shoulder presses hard on the warm little body beside her. She smells his milky breath, looking at how her muddy shoes have spoilt the white blanket. The hood's lacy edging frames the porch. Pearl settles herself more comfortably, thinking about her worms nicely lying in their rows, and waits for the front door to open.

Stream

The weeping willow Pearl is riding dips its neck into a clear, brown stream. Sssshhhh, she whispers, as she pats the bucking trunk and grips with her thighs. Above her, the willow tosses its shaggy arms. Slim, fish-shaped leaves fall past Pearl and plop into the stream. She dangles over to watch and inhales as the slivers of green swim away; the stream's breath smells of bright weeds, frogspawn, lichened pebbles. The water is a dazzling drink. Circular, swirling eyes come and go on its surface. Underneath, worm-thin plants all reach forwards, like hair in the wind. Pearl would love to be a stickleback, or a newt, and have the stream as her home. She climbs out of the tree and joins the tall fern-crowds running down to see the water. As she slips through they slap her with gentle, lemony hands, streaking her with juice. Pearl's shorts and pink sun-top all feel so stupid. She wades into the water, her sandals growing heavy, and waits for the stream to settle. Insects are ticking in the undergrowth. Kingcups glow amongst the fleshy plants along the water's margin. Pearl lies down in a smooth, shallow pool. Her hair entwines with the waving plants, her skin turns to liquid, her open eyes are just-born jewels. She can feel her brown limbs dissolving. Sunlight falls in bars and spots through the trees. As the lovely water laps her ears and throat, moves inside her shorts, slips across her fragile ribs, Pearl grins, thinking she hears laughter, and raises her arms to the just-glimpsed sky. These are some of the reasons she comes to the woods.

The Kerb

The ice-cream van has just driven out of the street; its tatty, fading tune makes Pearl feel bereft. She loves to stand by the juddering flank of the van and smell the petrol and vanilla it exhales. The smiling man made a towering cream cone for someone else, sprinkling it with coloured specks, squirting scarlet sauce from his old plastic bottle. Pearl wasn't tempted. Alone, she sits on the kerb and licks an apple ice-lolly. The dust in the gutter is sour and hot, and Pearl sees there is a beetle pulling a dead leaf through it. She picks him up and flings him onto the grass. While he sails through the air Pearl sees his jaws are still clamped to the leaf; it makes her want to smile. But still, it's samey, she thinks, how nothing ever happens in her street, and she sucks her lolly so powerfully the colour fades to ice. She drops a chunk inside her sundress, and feels it slither down to her belly button. Then Pearl senses an odd acceleration in the air. Her head feels as if someone has slipped a tight cap on it. Everything becomes empty and glowing, the sun obscured by mist. Pearl feels excited. She's stared at the sky so hard it seems bright pink, and the outlines of the garden hedges are black and twitching. She begins to laugh as the hairs on her arms rise. Heavy, warm raindrops splat like flicked spoonfuls of soup on Pearl's upturned face and bare shoulders. Lightning cracks above the rooftops, revealing the stunning light from a more interesting world behind the sky. Pearl drops her lolly in the dust, sits on the kerb and holds up her palms while racing clouds are reflected in her huge eyes.

Perfume

Pearl has been crouched in her cupboard. It smells of books and Plasticine, drying paintbrushes and the old wool kilt she hid long ago. As she sits cross-legged, Pearl can smell, amongst all these things, her own warm self. She puts her fingers inside her pants and dips them into the dense scalloped folds between her legs. Then she pulls her fingers out. Here is my smell, she thinks. I'm like the smashed roots of bluebells. She sniffs deeply. And the soft insides of baby hazelnuts. Then she crawls out of the cupboard and goes to her parents' room. On her mother's dressing table there are bottles and pots Pearl has never touched before. The sun can't get into this room; it's semi-dark even now, although Pearl knows it's the morning. She sits on the stool and looks at all her mother's things, then picks up a bottle and undoes the lid. It smells like her mother, and Pearl sneezes three times, her head nodding with each sneeze. She sniffs the tubes of scarlet lipstick, and the hairbrush. Even the cotton-wool balls in their glass jar smell the same. When she slides open the slim middle drawer, powdery air puffs up and makes her gag. She rummages amongst the silk fragments and lace underwear for a moment, then snatches her fingers away. In the tilted mirror she seems almost transparent. Pearl unfurls a lipstick and draws bold, red circles around her eyes and mouth. Then she makes faces in the mirror, her single, springy curl bobbing like a tiny, gilded horn. The white-covered bed stretches out, its edges crisp as a slab of stone. I love my own smell of bluebells and nuts, she thinks, crossing her eyes and making kissing sounds at her reflection.

Playing on the Stairs

Her parents are very firm about the stairs. How Pearl should hold the banister, place each foot just so, and absolutely no running. Pearl always listens to her parents. They're grown-ups, after all. She likes to sit on the sixth step and look up and down. She thinks about the stairs a lot; how they are not a room, but inside a house. And the stairwell shoots away, almost to the roof. Pearl plays with her brother on the landing. He isn't crawling yet. She's pulled him, tangled in a wisp of blanket, out of his cot and laid him on the edge of the top step. She uncovers his head and tells him that from now on, secretly, he will be called The Blob. Then she wraps him up again. Her mother is in the garden hanging out washing. From the sixth stair Pearl waits to see what will happen next. The Blob is cocooned in his shawl. He wobbles above her, then flops down onto the first step and bounces on its edge. Down he comes, one, two, three. By the time he hits four he's turned over. On the fifth step he falls onto his face and screams. The sound punches Pearl's ears and streaks jaggedly all around the stairwell. She lunges at the jerking bundle, clutches him tightly, stomps up to the room they share, then heaves him over the rail of his pale blue cot. He stops crying and begins to make an annoying, hiccupy sound. Pearl can see blood in his nostril, and the lashes of his screwed-up eyes are like fragments of black lace. She strokes his hot head for a second, then quietly shuts the bedroom door, creeps out of the house and goes to the woods.

Garden

Pearl has been busy with her tea set under the tall privet hedge that borders the back garden. Cream tapers of crumbly blossom poke out from the leaves, filling the air with a smell of wee and warm fudge. Under the hedge the shade flickers and buzzes. Pearl kneads some cakes out of damp mud, decorating them with insects she has caught. Some of the insects wriggle, so she presses them into the cakes until they lie quietly. From the kitchen Pearl can hear women's voices, and a radio playing. There is the sharp sound of laughter occasionally. She crouches, perfectly still, and watches as a girl steps out into the sunlight, crosses the lawn and walks close to the hedge. Just as she's about to go past, Pearl shoots out her hand, grabs the girl's bare ankle and yanks her down. Ouch, the girl says, on her knees, and acts as if she's about to cry. She's pale, with a sparse, floppy fringe and teeth you notice. Pearl pulls her into the den she's made. You're new, Pearl states. They look at the mud cakes. What are those? the girl asks. Yum, Pearl says. Eat one. She encloses the girl's pliant wrist with both hands and administers a Chinese burn. Eat one, she says, then I'll stop. Are those insects? the girl asks. Pearl goes on twisting. The girl bites into a cake. Her eyes run and snot seeps onto her upper lip. Pearl can hear crunching. The girl swallows, her big teeth muddy. Now you can get lost, Pearl says. But I want to stay, the girl whispers. Pearl expected this. Name? she asks. I'm Fee, the girl answers, settling comfortably, her limp wrist still lying in Pearl's brown hands. Now will you have me as your friend?

Potty

Strands of sun slant in through the kitchen window, drying the wooden draining board again. Already the hours feel old and exhausted. It's been cleaning day, and the house is filled with that lonely atmosphere of bleach and polish throughout. There is nowhere in the entire place she can go and be safe. Even the garden is unappealing; too open and bright, too raw and flat for her to play in. Pearl has sunburnt shoulders, the skin lifting off in airy petals she likes to eat. She drops her head as she stands in the doorway, feeling her cool cheek as it rests on the ragged skin, watching as their mother lowers her brother onto his potty. From the kitchen comes a beige-and-green cooking smell Pearl doesn't like, something she will be expected to eat later. The smell makes her feel as if she'd like to crumple today up and chuck it out, somewhere no one will ever think of looking. This feeling weakens her legs so they fold, and she plonks down on the cool tiles. The Blob is only wearing a skimpy vest. His fat bottom over-spills the potty rim. Both pink circles are distorted in the shining tiles. He is happily munching, fists holding a chocolate biscuit, his face smeared with melted brown goo. He has knobbly wet bits slicked in his hair and crusting his eyebrows. Even though Pearl knows it is only chocolate, her mouth fills with salty saliva and she begins to heave. She moves onto her hands and knees. Looking at her brother's toes, she sees the brown stuff is also on his feet and elbows. Pearl vomits all over her mother's slippery vermilion tiles.

Bunny

Pearl does a certain thing with her soft, pink toy rabbit. He's bald in places and has yellow buttons for eyes, and the insides of his floppy ears are made from a shiny fabric she likes to rub between her thumb and fingers. When Pearl was very little she discovered that if she pushed her rabbit up in the nook between her legs and squeezed him tight, then a lovely, lonely, secret feeling flooded from him into her, taking her breath away. Most people think how cute it is, the way Pearl will not be parted from her toy. No one knows about his special powers. Her father reads a story every night, mostly about good girls with straight fringes and striped dresses who help their mothers and are kind to pets, but at the moment they are reading *The Jungle Book*. Pearl thinks she could be the brother of Mowgli. That way, he would never pine to go back to the boring man-village; he'd have a person with him in the jungle whenever one was needed. The radiator clicks warmly and the curtains hang in even folds as she lies on the pillow, watching her father's mouth telling her about the wolf clan and the lonely hill they use as their home. His hands are holding the book in a way Pearl loves, and she is holding her pink bunny so he can follow things easily; his ears point upwards and his yellow buttons look over the top of the blanket. Then Pearl has an idea. She pulls her rabbit out and gives him to her father, who absent-mindedly holds him in his open palm as he reads. Pearl looks into the yellow buttons of her rabbit sitting there on her father's hand and soon she feels the familiar, luscious quiver her bunny always gives her.

Snow will fall

Pearl's father promises snow. She has absolute faith, but still the snow is reluctant. In the shed they pull down the sleigh with its metal runners, Pearl passes the oil and a rag for him to rub each curved, rusting length. Then they go out into the blasted winter garden and hold hands as he sniffs the air. Well, he says, and sniffs again. Pearl doesn't interrupt. Yes, he says, I think very soon, and he suddenly tightens his grip on her gloved hand. It feels like an electric shock leaping up Pearl's arm, he is so strong. Which day, Daddy? she asks. This weekend definitely, he says, and shocks her one more time. On Saturday the sky is porridge-coloured. Pearl imagines the blobs of snow teeming against each other as they get ready. She doesn't want to eat any lunch, even though her mother has made toast soldiers. The brown dotted egg smells funny. A banana has been waiting, curved around half her plate. She gags pointedly on it until her mother gives up and snatches it out of her slack fist. Then she goes to the park and settles herself on a swing. Pearl keeps her eyes shut. She wants to feel the snow first. She sits until her nose tip is wet and her feet are freezing. As the hours go by her hands in their woollen gloves meld to the swing chains. It begins to get dark. Pearl is pale, almost swooning with cold and hunger. The lamp lights come on but Pearl doesn't see them. Then, softly, softly, snowflakes touch her lips and eyelids and she leaps off the swing. Pearl twirls in the shifting, snow-bedazzled park until her red hat flies away and she falls down.

Bad

There's nothing to do. Pearl's friend Fee has gone on holiday. For weeks before she went, Pearl wouldn't speak to her. They still met every day of course. At first, Fee tried to explain about the place they always went for their holidays; about the sea, and camping, but Pearl wouldn't listen. On the evening before Fee left they were under the privet hedge in Pearl's garden. But why? Fee kept on asking. Why won't you speak, my love? Pearl sat cross-legged, picking a scab on her knee, her face set like a fierce, rosy mask. Fee tried to hold Pearl's hand. I can't help it, my parents are in charge, you know that, she told Pearl. They both watched blood ooze out from under the ripped scab. Pearl was silent. She pulled in her cheeks and made her lips like a cartoon fish. As Fee sobbed, Pearl put her own squished-up mouth on the wet, broken scab and sucked. Then she screamed at Fee with bloody lips and punched her in the stomach. Now Pearl looks out of her bedroom window at the children playing in the street, and rests her middle on the windowsill tiles. She can feel a chilly pulse in her belly that comes from her navel. The pulse seems to rise and sit in the tubes of her ears and the cave of her mouth. It's a wrong, blush-making feeling, but Pearl stays pressed against the sill, thinking of Fee, the way she'd looked after the punch, struggling to close her lips over her sticky-out front teeth. Pearl has known about this pulsing feeling and the windowsill for a long time, but she hated it so much she only did it once, till now. She is going to do it every day, until her best friend Fee comes back.

Scissors

Pearl is making a costume for the doll she was given as a birthday gift. Already the doll's got a blind eye, a missing hand and a severe haircut. Mostly it lies, splay-legged, under the bed. Pearl's found her mother's sharp scissors and is cutting an old jumper, but it won't keep still. She's thrown by how hopeless she is; even her mother snips through all sorts of things, all the time, without any trouble. Pearl begins to get more energetic. The Blob holds onto her armchair, watching her fight with the snarled-up wool. Bloody! she shouts, throwing the mess down and making him flinch. Do you see this stupid doll? she asks him as he loses his balance and sits down on the floor. I didn't want it. She stands over him and tells him that no one ever asks her what she wants. In fact, no one asks me anything, she says. The Blob sucks his thumb and plays with a carpet tuft. Then he wants to get on the chair so Pearl bunks him up. Immediately he starts to scream. She grabs him. Blood is blooming on her dress, leaking from his leg. Pearl slaps her hand over his mouth so violently he stops, and realises that a point of the scissors has gouged a lump of flesh from his bare thigh. She snatches bits of jumper, pressing, and looks around for something better. When she turns back the jumper is wet and scarlet. Her brother gulps, sucking his thumb, his eyes fixed on hers. Make a sound and you're dead, she says, and tucks him into the chair, covering him with a pile of material. Then she listens at the door. Now she is going to creep out and hide the scissors in the woods, then, maybe, later, come back home.

Punishment

As her mother screws a lock and bolt to Pearl's bedroom door she explains that, except for school, Pearl will not be allowed out until she considers what she has done wrong and apologises. The Blob whispers under the door as often as he can. Pearl thinks it's nice, lying with her ear to the gap, listening to his little baby-messages. If she squints she can see the bandage on his leg. She has curled her voice up in her throat, though, and sent it to sleep. In school she is so silent her teacher has even taken her into the Headmaster's office, but no one can get Pearl to utter a word. After a while she decides to eat only flat food like slices of cucumber and tomato, maybe crisps; things she doesn't have to open her mouth too wide for. After seven days her mother joins The Blob on the landing outside her bedroom. Pearl lies on her bed, arms behind her head, bare feet resting on the wall above the pillows. Her tummy feels scooped-out and her hip bones sharp. She hears her mother telling The Blob things he must repeat to her, but she no longer bothers to listen. Late one night she wakes to the sound of her mother unscrewing the lock and bolt. At the start of the second week Fee visits with a small plate of cheese slices and apple half-moons arranged like the petals of a flower. From your mother, my love, she says, placing them on the bedside table. Pearl closes her eyes and feels Fee lean over her. When's your Dad coming home? Fee asks, her thin, reddish hair falling onto Pearl's face as she kisses her pale lips. Four days' time, Pearl says. Then she's silent again.

A new thought

Pearl thinks about how she has only one grandmother. Fee has two, other children have two. She doesn't mind so much about not having grandads, but her one Gran is so nice, she would like another. She sits on the settee and feels the knobbly cushion under her thighs. Her father is reading the paper beside her. She looks at his crossed leg and brown shoe with its laces firmly tied, and the gap between his fawn sock and cord trouser. The skin she can see is darker than the sock, lightly covered with pretty brown hairs, and she can't stop herself reaching to touch. He puts the paper down. Are you tickling me? he asks, smiling. Yes, says Pearl, but really she knows that's not true. Daddy, she says, why have I only got one granny? Her father folds the paper and lifts her onto his lap. My mother would have been your other gran, he explains, while Pearl rests her head on his chest. But she's not here any more. Where is she then? Pearl says, although suddenly she almost knows. She's dead, her father says. She was ill, and then she died. And I was very sad. Pearl sits up straight. She feels a new idea taking shape in her head. It's amazing. Her father looks a little worried. But Pearl, he says, then you came along and cheered me up. You are my little star. Pearl smiles at her father and gives him a long hug. Now that's true, she thinks. I am star-ish. I have to get going, she says, giving him a kiss on his fragrant cheek. Then she slides down from her father's lap and runs out into the garden. In amongst the apple trees she feels so excited she wants to float like a balloon. So, mothers can die, she thinks, running from tree to tree. I never knew that.

Bus

There are some people sitting in front of Pearl and her mother, having a snack. Pearl leans over the back of their seat. As she is usually sick on any bus journey, the only thing her mother will give her is a mint, and her mother especially doesn't like it when Pearl looks at the other passengers too much. I don't know why you can't just look out of the window like everybody else, she says, manhandling Pearl into a suitable sitting position. But these people are opening bags of salted nuts, and nibbling pastries. Pearl twists out of her mother's grip, climbs down off her seat and edges around so that she's standing next to the woman, watching as another damp parcel is unwrapped. Pearl sees there are little sandwiches inside. She wonders what sort. She likes ham, or lemon curd, or sometimes, golden syrup in her sandwiches. She takes a good look; they are grated cheese. That's her favourite. Her eyes follow every movement as the woman and her friend lift the food to their mouths. They chew like robots. Eventually, there is only one delicious square left, and Pearl announces that she really loves cheese sandwiches. She pushes against the woman's thigh as she says it, and holds out her hand. But no one takes any notice of Pearl. The woman packs the last sandwich away, takes an apple and crunches it. Specks of spit fly out of her mouth. Pearl's mother takes hold of her arm and says, before you start you can stop, or else, but Pearl is not ready. First, in a firm voice, she tells the people that she hates them. And as her mother pulls her arm Pearl adds that she hopes they both choke.

A good plan

Pearl stands on the bank and looks across to a beach-like area the cows have trampled as they come to drink. Hazy clouds of greenery are reflected in the water. It feels like an island over there, with its alder trees and yellow lilies, the canal curving around, but she knows it isn't. She lies down on the fringe of the canal and dabbles in the slow water. Just out of reach Pearl can see, resting on the bottom, masses of cloudy, dotted frogspawn. She lowers her chin onto her folded arms and concentrates on it. Each tiny, opaque, black-centred globe is like an eye, and all the eyes are looking her way. Every year she collects buckets of spawn and takes it home to the garden. She can never resist feeling the jelly, combing it again and again. She thinks about her buckets and nets, her plan to take frogspawn home. Even though she enjoys arranging shiny weeds in amongst it, and little sparkly stones, she sees now it's not a good idea. Her beautiful spawn always changes and dies. After a while, she decides to catch tiddlers instead. Pearl enjoys wading, and jumps a little each time a plant twines around her ankles. But still the buckets remain empty. It feels better, somehow, to leave the quiet spawn and flickering fish alone, here in the cool, barely moving water. Pearl sits on the bank and tries to pick a bunch of kingcups. Their stretchy stems squeak and colour her hands, but she cannot pull them out. Pearl rests in the gnat-rich air, feeling the grass tickling her legs, then gathers all her things. She has decided nothing is leaving the canal today.

New friend

It's the summer holidays. Pearl has been thinking how all the long, sunny days rest closely up against each other like leaves in a huge book about dust, heat, melting pavements. Today she is going to rip out a page and see what happens. She tries to imagine the winter, and yearns for gloves and steady, slashing rain, even stew. There is a new girl in the street and Pearl has to find some things out. The girl's called Honey. That's not a proper name, Pearl says, when they meet for the first time under the hedge; it's something you put on bread. She sits astride Honey's stomach, pins her arms down and leans over. I'll do something bad if you don't do what I tell you to do, she says. Honey's eyes are hazel, and her lashes are thick and auburn. Open up, Pearl tells her, and points to Honey's lips. Wider, Pearl shouts, wide, wide, wide! Honey has strong, square teeth, and her lips stretch as if she is laughing. Pearl gathers spit with her tongue and allows it to fall in a series of slow bubbles into Honey's mouth. Now swallow, she tells her, or else. Then she lets her up. Can I do you now? Honey asks. Nope, Pearl says. They kneel and face each other. Honey starts to play with the worm casts all around them. Okay, she murmurs, and squeezes a blob of mud in her palms. Pearl watches as she fashions the mud into a little shape. Hold out your hand, she tells Pearl. She has made a mud dog. Pearl studies Honey's perfect pink cheeks and extraordinary lashes. This could work out, she thinks, cradling the brown mini-creature in her hands.

No

Pearl switches off as she pushes the shopping trolley past the cooked ham and cheese counters. With her mother walking beside her holding on, she begins to imagine what it would be like to stay in the supermarket after closing time. She'd build a tent of cereal boxes and find matches and magazines to make a fire. Then she'd cook sausages and, for afters, eat chocolate with nuts inside. Pearl glances at her mother, who's in her slippers, nightdress billowing out from her half-undone coat. Pearl thinks the filmy pink fabric looks rude in the shop. As her mother picks up a bag of sugar, Pearl can hear her talking in an undertone, asking the sugar questions. In her tent Pearl would light candles and lie down amongst a pile of cushions. She pictures the glow from inside lighting up the tall canyon of tins she's below. Pearl lets go of the trolley and slinks off as her mother cradles the sugar and sings to it; the little song fades as Pearl turns in to another aisle. All the shoppers silently walk around, turning their heads from side to side, and Pearl is invisible. She could also climb up the shelves and stand on the top, she thinks, maybe even jump from one stack to another, all alone in the dark of the huge, crammed warehouse. Soon she hears screams. Nothing can stop them, Pearl knows. She weaves through the crowd and sees first a pink slipper yawning on the tiles, and then her mother struggling with a person in uniform. She's screaming because he wants to take her sugar-baby from her. Pearl stands mutely until someone asks if this is her mother. Then she backs away, shaking her head.

43

Clump

The kids in the next street have been making an obstacle course in a thick hedge that grows all along the top of a bank. Pearl watches, perched on her bike, until the two boys in charge come over. You're Pearl, aren't you? one asks. The boys are holding interesting garden implements. She circles round them silently while they whisper together. You can join, if you like, the boy waving a pair of shears says. Pearl runs through the suitable stuff in her father's shed. Maybe I will, she calls over her shoulder as she rides off. Now, every day in the summer holidays, she's hard at it, and her part of the hedge run is going well. She's constructing a ramp you can pelt up and jump off into a soft pit of grass. Today she's stripping hazel boughs with her penknife when someone shouts that her brother's in a fight. Pearl folds her knife, and lays the branches in a heap. Where? she asks, and rides off, standing on the bike pedals. At the playground she parks and has a look. Pearl sort of knows the boy who is punching her brother. Quietly she walks up behind him as he stoops over The Blob and leaps onto his back, hooking her legs around his waist. He whirls and staggers, trying to grab her, while she pulls his head back by the hair and yanks until a wet, tufty clump of scalp comes away in her fist. The boy collapses backwards, on top of her. Want some more? she shouts, as he scrambles up, grunting, and runs away. She gives her brother a long look while putting the clump in her shorts pocket. Then she rides back to the ramp and hazels, her hair flowing behind her like a small silken flag.

Smile

Pearl and her brother are banished to the carpetless back bedroom. A rickety playpen sits in the middle of the room, full of boxes and broken lampshades. Pearl can see they would make a really good den but she can't be bothered. Their mother has said Pearl is in trouble; one more thing and she won't be responsible. Now Pearl is thinking about how The Blob's stupid face deserves a slap. She must make something happen anyway. He's pushing a toy car around, making a private brumming noise as he drives it over the swirls in the carpet. These bits are the roads, he tells Pearl. Who cares about the stupid roads? Pearl says. Her brother gives her a wary look. In fact, who cares about you at all? she asks him, putting her face up close. No one in this house. I heard Mother say she prayed you'd be run over by a lorry. Her brother starts to grizzle, and Pearl snatches his car, throwing it against the wall. Now what you going to do? she shrieks. The Blob runs down to the kitchen, wailing. Pearl sits on the floor and waits, her fingers quiet, for what will happen next. After a few moments, her mother runs heavily up the stairs and appears in the doorway. And here we go, Pearl thinks, watching her mother shout. Pearl doesn't listen; she studies her mother's scarlet face and spitting mouth, the way she clenches her hands and glares. Best of all, the veins in her mother's neck start to bulge like shuddering blue worms. What have you got to say for yourself, you horrible little thing? her mother yells. Pearl lowers her eyes, soft hands in her lap, but it's hard, keeping a straight face.

Upside down

Pearl and Fee gaze from the open bedroom window; the field has vanished, trees thrash and the sky above the jerking branches is ominous. They try to stretch their bare arms out into the storm. A soft roar fills the warm room, but the rain doesn't touch them. Pearl throws some of her best things as far as she can out into the downpour. She wants to go stream-wading, and shuts her eyes to watch herself struggling through the saturated ferns, feeling with wet fingers the little raised buttons on the fern fronds' undersides. She knows the clear brown water of the stream will be mixing with transparent snakes of rain. She longs to feel her wellies slap against her legs. It's too dry in this place, she tells Fee. Inside my nose itches. No, Fee says, bouncing on the bed, please let's stay here. It's cosy and safe. Then she lands awkwardly and falls down between the bed and the wall. Pearl sighs, looking at the treetops. I know what we can play, Fee says, her voice muffled, Upside Down! There are two beds in Pearl's room. Fee has The Blob's. Each girl lies on her back across one and drops her head over the side so she is looking at the other the wrong way up; where a forehead should be, there is a mouth; instead of a chin, two spidery eyes. They laugh in the thrumming room. Pearl thinks Fee's mouth looks like a dark hole; the uneven row of teeth decorating the edges is the best thing ever. Then Fee stretches out to stroke Pearl's cheek. I expect you've forgotten all about the stream now, my love, she says, smiling. Pearl sits up and shakes herself. No, she answers. I absolutely have not.

Break

There's a boy in Pearl's class who's broken his arm. Pearl watches as he uses the plaster cast for all sorts of useful jobs. And he tells everybody he can't really go in the bath, because he has to keep the plaster dry. The children all laugh when he slides a ruler inside to scratch, and flock around him, waiting their turn to write a funny message on the white plaster. But Pearl keeps her distance. Still, the thought of the cast fascinates her. By the time she and Fee walk home through the park, Pearl is silent, thinking about the way his four fingers curl themselves from the hard shell, and how his thumb pokes out at a different angle to how you would have imagined. She shakes her head when Fee wants to go on the swings. At the tea table she refuses to eat, but only after everyone has finished can Pearl go out through the front door, across the field and down the bank. Without stopping she jumps over the stream and shoulders her way through the undergrowth until she's at the foot of her favourite tree. She squats in a fork of exposed root, listening to the evening birds and insects, not thinking of anything. Finally she starts to climb. This tree has limbs that rise like steps all around its lower trunk, and Pearl moves up quickly. She feels light and full of air, her legs strong. Soon it gets more difficult, and she's hot, hauling herself up, holding the gnarly wood, her knees trembling. Still she climbs until she's through the leaves and clinging to the tree's topmost, whippy branches. Faintly, she can hear her father calling her in to bed. I'm coming, Daddy! she yells, and jumps.

Pat

Pearl is back in her own room. Now, after the ambulance, the hospital, all the fuss and shouting, she feels different; as thin and hard as a pin, maybe, or flat and cold like a paving stone. Not like a living girl any more. Her father stands at the foot of the bed concentrating, his hand jangling the keys in his pocket, while her mother, stroking the cast on Pearl's leg, perches so close that her perfume spreads all over the bed. Pearl watches, perfectly still and hardly breathing. Up and down goes her mother's white hand with its wedding ring, up and down. One perfect, yellow curl sits stiffly on her forehead. It's horrible, so Pearl closes her eyes. Inside, she is shivering with a desire to scream at her mother to get out! get out! The feeling is so powerful she must be giving off scorching rays. But no. Still stroking the plaster, finally her mother starts to speak. I know all about you, Pearl, she says. I was a little girl once. I had a sister, and a mother and father. Pearl hears the tears in her mother's voice and opens her eyes a fraction. On she goes, about how she cares for Pearl. Unlike her voice, her eyes are hard and shining, as if they're stretching out of their sockets, and her lips are pursed. She says how upset she was when Pearl fell from the tree. Then she pecks Pearl on the forehead, mouth bunched so tight it's like a painful flick, and leaves. The things her mother said press Pearl into the mattress. Now, see? her father says, relaxing his brows as he sits for a moment beside her. Can't you tell how much your mother loves you? He looks so sweet, Pearl makes a huge effort to smile and pat his hand.

Rebirth

Pearl thinks about her leg inside its lumpy plaster cast. How it must be growing strong, like a pale, sturdy root does, in the dark. She has been patient, all these weeks, and silent, even when needles of pain jabbed her. Today the cast will be removed. It feels like a huge thing is about to happen. Her aunty takes her to the hospital. Pearl is glad; her aunty is comfortable, and doesn't expect anything. When they get there, Pearl is so excited, she feels as if her whole body is shimmering with white light. Don't be nervous, her aunty says, patting her hands. There's absolutely nothing to worry about. Then she examines Pearl's face. But you're not frightened, are you? Pearl shakes her head. You are a funny little thing. Pearl nods from where she lies on the couch and watches the nurse use a little instrument with a whirring blade to cut through the thick cast. White powder flies around, and then Pearl sees the nurse force apart the crumbling shell. Suddenly, the cast looks old and fragile. And there is Pearl's new leg, all covered in wisps of bandage and fluff. The nurse uses a wet cloth to wipe it clean. Pearl can see strange pink signs on her shin, and remembers the bone splintering through. She examines her leg. As good as new, her aunty says, stroking her back. Pearl is silent. She knows her leg is better than new. She is even more beautiful now, with the marks like a secret message only she can read. Up she gets from the bed. Can I go? she asks, limping to the door. She wants to run and run and never stop.

Tears

When Pearl gets home from school, the front door is ajar and in the kitchen nothing's on the table, just a bowl of wrinkled apples. Where's my snack? she shouts, and throws her bag down. She's so hungry her hands are sweating. Then she sees smashed china on the floor, and across the wall a long, streaky stain. Pearl's scalp begins to tingle; the house feels wrong. From upstairs she can just make out a rumble of voices. She tiptoes to the hall and waits. Her father appears on the landing and after him, a strange man. When they come down the stairs Pearl hides and peeps out as the man shakes her father's hand and leaves. She decides to stay hidden, and when the coast is clear, grab some food and go to the woods, but her father stands in the hall and doesn't move. Pearl sees how his hand rests on the doorknob, and she frowns, watching the nerveless way he eventually lets go and allows his arm to drop to his side. He's not his usual, substantial self. Now she understands. Her mother is ill again, and that man was the special doctor. Pearl feels her chest emptying; everything will be ruined now. The house has turned itself inside out. She realises with a jolt her father has gone, though she didn't see him move. She picks up a jagged chunk of plate. There are sounds from the lounge and she hides again. With the chunk she scrapes a note to herself on the back of the kitchen door. Then she creeps out and looks into the lounge. There is her father with his hands hiding his face. His shoulders are moving. Oh no, Daddy, she cries, and runs to embrace him.

Mixed up

Pearl is staying at Aunty Betty's. She loves the spicy, untidy kitchen, and the way her aunty darts round, always knowing where every little thing is. Yes, I'm your mother's sister, she explains. But Pearl still thinks her mother could never have a sister; it feels impossible. She gazes with narrowed eyes while her aunt continues to flash a knife through potatoes, trying to catch a glimpse of her mother in her aunty's smiling face. I don't think I believe you, Aunty Betty, Pearl says politely. Her aunty kisses her cheek and shoos her out of the kitchen. She climbs the wide wall that surrounds the garden to sit on a comfortable, sun-warmed stone. The world's confusing, she thinks. Raspberry-coloured valerian fizzes out from the cracks below like mad eyelashes, and a creeping plant with round leaves is inching its way over the surface of the wall. Pearl fingers a hairy, coin-shaped leaf. It's just the same as the belly skin of a hamster. Most things are like something else, she thinks. But her mother's not like anyone. Then she realises that these plants think the wall is the earth; and she doesn't blame them. On her front she hangs her head over the edge. Below her, on the ground at the base of the wall, spreads a pool of sky-blue flowers. From this angle Pearl is seeing down the wall, through the plants that sprout from it and on into the billowy blueness. After looking and looking she gets mixed up, and starts to feel as if she's pinned to a forgotten surface. So, she wonders sleepily, am I looking the right way? Where exactly is the sky? And where is the earth?

Glad

Pearl is sitting cross-legged in School Assembly. A mass of children sway to another stupid song, and Pearl is looking about, trying to find something. She scans along the huge curtains that flank one wall, and there amongst the folds and big blue roosters she sees, for the first time, the little skeleton girl. Over the heads of the fidgeting children Pearl gazes into the eye sockets of the skeleton girl, who holds the curtain out of the way with her bone hand and smiles back with long teeth. Then she points at Pearl with one finger and lets the curtain fall. Through Spelling and English, and when her teacher tells a story, Pearl keeps looking around the classroom. In the canteen, sitting amongst the plastic plates of uneaten dinner and the shouting children, she thinks maybe she's caught a glimpse of the girl hanging quietly from the rafters, but she knows she's mistaken. After school, Pearl walks quickly, but doesn't go home. She sits by the stream, dabbles her feet and thinks. There is a minty perfume in the dim, mobile air. As she gazes across the shallow water into the ferns, she realises the skeleton girl is there, watching. Pearl listens to the clink of bones as the girl walks down the bank and folds with a clatter into the sludge and shale on the opposite side of the stream. Through the girl's ribs Pearl can see ferns trembling. In the stream Pearl's feet look grey, and so do the fanned-out bones of the skeleton girl's feet. Pearl doesn't say a thing when the girl drops her head to one side and splashes her stick legs in the water. She's just glad the skeleton girl is with her now.

Sandwiches

It's always nicer when Pearl's mother is not at home. The Blob and Pearl are friends then, and help their father in the garden. This evening The Blob plays with his cars, but Pearl is hard at work digging with a spade, and later, riddling rough earth. Look, Daddy, she calls, holding up a big circular riddle with its heap of captured stones until he notices and says she's his good girl. Pearl walks between the tall runner-bean aisles, smelling the plants and searching for earwig horns that poke out from the scarlet flowers. Her father clears the ground and throws weeds and garden rubbish in a heap. After the fire is lit he calls the children to sit and listen to it hiss and sing, but the smoke always makes Pearl hungry. The evening blackbirds calling to each other from the row of watchful trees are so sad she ends up hugging her father's leg until he can't work any more. Then they all go into the kitchen and prepare the plants he's thinned out of the vegetable rows. I'll be mother, Pearl says, tying on a big apron, and sets about splashing cold water over them in the sink; wispy carrots, soft, heartless florets of lettuce and, best of all, wands of spring onions, their bulbs slippery, eyeball-white. With chilled hands Pearl first shares out the tiny carrots. Father slices thick hunks of bread, butters them, then piles on the tender lettuces and onions and rains down salt. He puts more bread on top and cuts the whole thing into four squares. On the side of their plates sit cubes of cheese. In the evening light, Pearl and her brother smile at each other over the juicy, green-filled, oniony sandwiches.

The claw

Pearl hates birthday parties. Here's your pretty dress and ribbons, her mother says, holding up a flounced, white frock embroidered with navy stars. Look at these sweet shoes I bought you. She's home again, and trying to be nice. But Pearl lies on the floor singing la-la, la-la, la-la, using just two notes, while her mother stands with the outfit in her spread arms. Pearl's hair will not behave. Her mother gets upset, messing with the cow's lick and curl, wetting it, clipping. This thing, she mutters. It just won't stay put. When she's ready, Pearl hunkers down, the puffy dress spread out. Everything she wears is disgusting, she tells her mother; then she jumps up and gallops off. Her brother hides, but Pearl finds him in the understairs cupboard and drags him out. He's holding his squashy, bald tiger. Give, shouts Pearl, but he hides it behind his back. Pearl draws in her lips. You will be sorry, she hisses through bared teeth. He begins to cry. I'm counting to three, she says, then it's The Claw for you, matey. Pearl's brother furrows his brow and juts his lower lip. Oh no, I'm so sc-sc-scared, she says, glad he won't hand over his tiger. Right you little nit, she whispers, and raises one hand, stiffening the thumb and fingers inwards, then grabs his cheeks and squeezes her fingers together. Feel The Claw, she yells, her silver curl bouncing free. Her brother's face is crunched between his upper and lower teeth. He wriggles, but her grip is strong and each move hurts him. Then she lets go; she's had a good idea. Later, she will go up to the stupid birthday girl, there amongst the sickening jelly and balloons, and do The Claw on her.

Pretend

There are soft mounds of newly mown grass on the field. Fee and Pearl gather armfuls for the walls of a house. They need a kitchen and lounge. You be father, Pearl tells Fee. I will be the kind, beautiful mother. She considers, her face almost obscured by fragrant, loose grass. No, you be my child, she says. Fathers are never there when you need them. Fee thinks she'll be a baby, but Pearl says, be a girl about your own age. Okay, says Fee, that's easy; I am a girl my own age. Pearl shakes out a layer of grass for the lounge carpet. Yes, but you'll be a *pretend girl*, she states. Okay, my love, Fee says. She knows Pearl hates explaining games too much. They go on being mother and child, and time passes. I must say, you are a very good child, Pearl says, rearranging Fee's straggly hair. Now wait there, she adds, pointing to a grass chair. And no, sshhh, she says, when Fee opens her mouth; little ones should be quiet. Pearl disappears, and when she gets back she's carrying a bag. Now it's dinner, she announces, kissing Fee's cheeks and tidying her dress. They sit and Pearl spreads a tea towel, placing on it an orange, dried prunes and a ham-and-egg pie. Fee contemplates the pie. Pearl, she says, won't your mother be angry you've stolen her food? Pearl doesn't answer. Instead she shares the picnic out. Nibbling prunes, she watches Fee eating half of the pie. Isn't that nice, my treasure? she asks, smiling. I'm sure you'd like more. So Fee eats the other half. Thank you, Mummy, Fee says. Pearl is busy peeling the orange. I think you're a lovely mother, Fee tells her. Really? Pearl asks, am I?

Click

Walkies! Pearl's mother calls. She makes them stand up straight in the hallway. Hands by your sides! she commands. Then she explains that only Pearl is allowed out. Her brother has to stay and guard the house. He couldn't even guard his bottle of milk, Pearl thinks. He's too little. And he'll be scared all alone. I'm the boss of you both, their mother says, picking up her purse and holding the door open for Pearl. You out, you in, she points at them in turn. The Blob's chin trembles and he stares hard at Pearl. Don't touch anything, she calls back as she's dragged into the windy afternoon. I'll think of a plan! Outside, it seems to Pearl that the birds are being hurled about the sky like small, feathered stones. Her mother's hair is spiky and the wind has slapped a makeshift red smile on her white face. Come along you, she shouts. Stop dawdling. I'm following my nose, and it won't wait for ever. On they go, Pearl hunched against the cold and her mother striding out, throwing her purse into the air and catching it like a sporty girl. When Pearl thinks about her brother and his trembling chin, something pings inside her skull. She looks at her mother's back and the pinging gets louder. From the tips of her fingers, jets of fire arc out towards her mother's head. Stop that or else, her mother says calmly, without looking round. Cars blare past while they wait to cross the road. Pearl hears one final loud click as she sees the skeleton girl nodding her skull amongst the pink flowers in the hedgerow opposite. Then, in blessed silence, she slips behind her mother and gets ready to shove.

Flight

Ever since the traffic incident with her mother, Pearl has been in her father's bad books. She tripped, I expect, he'd said to Pearl's mother, after she'd dragged Pearl home. Gently pulling her onto his knee, he'd asked Pearl if it was an accident. But she wouldn't answer, even though her heart was about to break out from her chest and flop like an almost dead fish down to the rug. After a short while he'd squeezed her hands and said, go to your room. I can't look at you. Pearl's legs felt as if they were filled with some heavy liquid. The stairs towered above her. To climb them she had to use her hands and knees. Now she doesn't want to come out of her room ever again. She pokes her tongue between her upper lip and front teeth, and even there it's cold. Every time she thinks of how her daddy said he didn't want to look at her she dry-sobs. Finally she realises the sun is shining, and so she climbs out of the window. Dropping lightly to the porch, she scrambles down the wall, grazing her knees. Deep in the flickering woods she struggles amongst the ferns, makes a burrow and falls asleep. She dreams that the roof of her mouth is crammed with innumerable grubs. It feels as if they are packed deep inside her head, growing fat. Clouds travel the sky and rain falls on her. Birds hop across her chest, grass grows between her toes. Underneath her knees insects make their homes. Then comes the moment when thousands of tiny blue butterflies fly out from her mouth in dazzling ribbons. As Pearl watches them merge with the sky, she thinks she hears her father's voice.

Pretty girl

There are lots of different reasons why Pearl wants to stay in her bedroom for ever. She likes to close the curtains and turn her bedside lamp on. In the pink glow she often presses her back to the radiator until she can't bear the heat a single second more. Or she'll lie on the floor under the bed, very still, waiting until the room settles and forgets she's there. Today she's exploring her cupboard, finding old things she'd lost or spoilt. There's a box on a high shelf, and as she pulls it down, flowery dresses and sun hats she half remembers tumble out in a series of soft sighs. Looking at the tangled heap of clothes makes her slump on the floor and think of nothing. After a while she realises her skeleton girl is propped against the bedroom door. It's difficult to know how her girl feels; she always smiles, come what may. Grabbing her twiggy little hands Pearl stands her upright. Then she begins to force her into a dress. It's tricky and noisy, but she keeps going. When all the buttons are done and the flounces are airy, she stands back. The skeleton girl looks like a collection of snapped branches with rags caught on them. Well, what a pretty girl you are, Pearl says in a made-up voice, looking at the dress with its smocking and frilly white collar. And doesn't this colour look sweet on you? Mmmm? Everyone will simply love you in this. The dress has yellow rosebuds and trailing green stems all over it. She scrabbles amongst the things on the floor for a hat. Dresses always looked stupid on me, she says, plonking a sunhat on her girl's smooth, bleached head, but I can see they make you very happy.

73

Love

Pearl has made a racing car out of the push-along wheelbarrow, some boxes and a bike wheel. It's a sunny afternoon, and she and The Blob have been sent out to play in the back garden. No one, absolutely no one, is allowed in this house, their mother says. What if I'm thirsty? Pearl asks, arms folded. What if I need the toilet? Pearl's mother hands her a plastic container filled with water. Share, she says, and wee under the hedge if you have to. Then she shuts the back door on them. Pearl settles in the cockpit of her car and pretends to drive. Her brother is digging with his little red spade. Carefully, he's filling a blue bucket with dry earth. That bucket's mine, Pearl thinks, and is about to jump out of her car to smack him for using her things when she notices that he's missing the bucket entirely and emptying his heaped spade over the side. He is so intent on digging that he doesn't notice. A far-off dog barks and Pearl sits, watching her brother in his sun hat as he digs away, singing to himself. She sees his bare, suntanned feet in his sandals, his dirty, rucked-up-at-the-back striped T-shirt and something happens to her eyes, something dark and hard shifts inside her chest. She feels it melting into something altogether different. She blinks and straightens her back. Come here! she calls sternly, and her brother jumps up immediately, looks around for his squashy tiger and runs to the front of the racing car. Want to come for a spin? she asks. As he clambers in behind her she passes him the water bottle. Hold on! she shouts. Ready? Then we're off!

Mothers and fathers

Honey and Fee are peeping through the stage curtains at the audience. Rehearsals have taken weeks, and tonight they do the play. What's so interesting? Pearl calls. The two girls gaze at her. She is dressed in the most amazing costume. Pearl, you look beautiful, Fee says, and runs to hold her hand. Aren't you scared? Honey asks. You have the most lines. Pearl is calm and silent. Don't you want to see your mum and dad? Fee asks. Come on, take a look. But Pearl shakes her head. Your mother is the most lovely of all the mothers, Honey tells her. She doesn't look like a mother at all, really. Or your father like a dad, Fee adds. Then a teacher calls and they run off. Pearl, in all her finery, walks to the curtains and puts an eye to the gap. She finds Honey's mother in the crowd; she has a soft shape. Segments of pink scalp show through Honey's father's hair. A few rows back, Fee's mum sits alone. She is pale and freckled, like Fee. Pearl watches as she opens a little case and puts her glasses on to study the programme. Pearl can almost imagine climbing onto her lap. It's true, she thinks. They all look cosy. Pearl knows exactly where her own parents are. It's as if a spotlight picks them out. There is her mother, in a red dress and red lips. Her blonde hair is glossy and waved. Pearl can see a glowing blob at each of her earlobes. They are her earrings. As Pearl watches she raises a white, scarlet-tipped hand to her hair. Beside her, Pearl's father sits, his dark suit absorbing light, his black hair crisp. Pearl moves back from the curtain. She's glad her mother and father don't look like anybody else's parents.

Watching

As Pearl walks through the empty village halfway up the mountain she gets a feeling someone is watching, so she twirls, scanning the windows and empty doorways of the cottages. Oi you! she calls, hands on hips. The silence is split by the coughing of startled sheep. Two crows stop jabbing their beaks at a bunch of purple thistle heads and look at her. The mountain's herby breath kisses her cheeks and cools her eyelids. From the scrubby square on the mountain's shoulder she can see down the valley, and there is her house, smaller than a fingernail. It's hard to imagine her mother banging about inside those tiny rooms, looking for Pearl. For a moment she tries to picture her little box of a room, with her bunny under the pillow and her cupboard full of secrets. On she goes, up past the forestry, past the smooth, gleaming reservoir, and on to the place where a huge cliff face swells from the ferns and whinberry bushes. She starts to climb, her legs and arms scratched by sharp plants. An enormous silence presses Pearl to the cliff. When she heaves herself onto the wide ledge that spreads out nearly at the top, she is surprised to see the skeleton girl. Have you been watching me? Pearl asks her. Then she sees the skeleton girl is holding up a sheep's skull, and working the jaws so that they bang open and shut. The long, bleached-out head is so heavy it wobbles in the skeleton girl's grey little claws. Pearl can't help laughing, it's so nice; the two smiling skulls, and the hollow clap of jaws ricocheting around the mountainside.

Different

Pearl and her granny are sitting in easy chairs opposite each other. On a small table are plates of toast and mugs of tea. In front of them, the fire has eaten the heart out of each rounded black-and-red coal in the grate, but still the fire is piled up, keeping its shape. Hungry flame-tongues slip through the dark slits where each coal rests against another. Pearl has been staring into the fire, watching as tiny glowing cities appear and fade, appear and fade. She rests her chin on her drawn-up knees and feels the wires that tightly hold her in place give a little, so she can move more easily and be calm. I see the fire-cities, she says. I see turrets and towers, stairways and doorways, lots of little dark windows. Mmmm, her gran says sleepily. Yes, those wonderful cities. Pearl can't take her eyes off the fire. She's imagining herself down there as a semi-molten person, changing colour and shape constantly; maybe a knight, or an orange horse, the size of a grain of rice, with a burning mane. Or, even better, a sleek, ash-scaled dragon, draped over the city's rooftops, scaring everybody. She rubs her eyes and looks at her grandmother. She has a question. Well, my Pearlywhirl, her gran asks. Out with it. Pearl already knows the answer, but she wants to hear the words. So, Grannywan, she says, stretching her arms slowly above her head, her cheeks pink, her big eyes glowing with red embers, was Mother like me when she was a child? Her grandmother considers. No. You and your mother are not alike in any way, she says finally.

Zip it

Pearl is stretched out on the settee, doing nothing. It's a thin, shivery kind of springtime, and outside the daffodils in the sloping lawn bob their heads above clumps of juddering leaves. This is exactly the kind of evening Pearl can't stand. It will be light for hours, and the way the birds in the garden call to one another makes Pearl think they hate it too. Her mother leans forwards in the chair opposite, sewing, straining to see her work in the grudging light. The Blob is building a fortress with wooden blocks. Every time he gets a wall how he likes it, Pearl knocks it down with her foot. Then he builds it again. Why don't you move your stupid wall away from me? she asks. You are so shtoopid, I almost feel sorry for you. Then she knocks it down again. Each time the bricks fall, their mother flinches. Pearl goes on talking to her brother and he listens, busy with his bricks. If you were a bit cleverer, she says, you'd have a fortress finished by now. But you wouldn't be The Blob if you did that, would you? He unhurriedly gathers his bricks and starts again. Pearl begins to sing a variation on her two-note song; shtoo-pid, shmoo-pid, shloo-pid, shkloo-pid. She can see her brother beginning to smile, so she sings a little louder, over and over. Then she stops singing mid-word and watches her mother slowly stand up, holding a short black zip in one hand and a needle and thread in the other. As her mother walks through the half-built bricks towards Pearl, she waves the zip and says, Ha! I've finally thought of a way to shut you up. Then she stumbles over a brick. Just you try singing then, Pearl, she says.

Crying

Pearl cries in the woods. At last she starts to hiccup and look around. Tender, wonky caterpillars are swaying from invisible threads. The sun is jabbing through the foliage like knitting needles, pointing out beautiful things. Bursts of golden light dart and pool in amongst the leaves. Her eyes are sore and swollen. Everything has a pink tinge. It's weird, and the woods start to look wrong, so she throws her voice up to the trees' heads. There's no reply as she walks back along the winding path, hiccuping quietly, and goes home. The houses in the street feel empty, and Pearl wonders where the neighbours could have gone. On the step she is reluctant to open the front door. Outside feels so airy. There are people somewhere doing normal things; shopping, walking their dogs, talking to each other. She turns the handle and there, drenched in a haze of bleach and polish, is her mother, on her knees, scrubbing the tiles, humming to herself. She breaks off to look at Pearl, then gets back to her work. She doesn't notice Pearl has been crying. In her bedroom Pearl looks in the mirror. The face reflected is like someone else's face; shiny, dark lips, drawn-down at the corners and a gruesomely running nose. But her eyes are the worst; the whites and irises are scarlet and the pupils tiny. It's terrifying, the way she looks. Pearl cries again, while the face in the mirror contorts, dripping uncontrollably. Pearl stares into her own eyes and thinks someone else is peering out through them. Her real self has leaked away. Now all that is left is this stranger, almost as unhappy as she is.

TV and nibbles

Pearl's parents are engrossed in themselves, dressing up in special clothes to go out. Her mother's blonde hair is done in soft bubbles. At her dressing-table mirror she applies lipstick while Pearl stretches on the huge bed. When her mother's lips are red she looks like a cruel woman in a book. Her neck and shoulders gradually drain of colour. Bubbles, white skin and the slash of scarlet; that's all there is. Pearl lies on her side and breathes quickly at the way her mother looks. Her dress is like a luminous skin, her shape all unfamiliar curves. Really, though, her father is the best; a tall, slender pillar of fluid black. His nose and mouth ready to go out somewhere Pearl doesn't know about. His dark hair burnished, his eyes blank and gleaming. The smell of his skin is sharp and grown-up. She wraps her arms around his legs and he laughs. I can't take you or your brother with me, he says, you would be bored, and tweaks her nose. Pearl knows that is not true. She has to struggle with her mouth, to keep it straight, when she leaves them to go to the babysitter's house. The TV is on, and she sips the Coke and eats a handful of the nuts laid out for her. There is a man reading the newspaper as Pearl perches on the edge of the settee. She is feeling strange because of the unfamiliar food. After some time the man peers over the top of the big, floppy pages. Where's your mother? he says. Pearl can't say exactly where. He bulges his eyes and rolls them round. She's gone off with a black man, he whispers, laughing silently at Pearl. Turning back to the TV she says, I know that, stupid.

Baking

When Pearl arrives at her grandmother's house, she makes straight for the dim front room. She loves the squat, wheezy clock on the mantelpiece, the horsehair settee, the sugary smell of ripening pears and the locked glass cabinet. Inside is a figurine; a girl with red cheeks and a black pleated skirt that lifts to show frilly knickers. Her plaid scarf flies backwards as she skims across a sheet of ice. Pearl smiles at the three-inch skating girl, whose teeth smile back. She stands quietly until her mother calls her from the kitchen. Pearl and her grandmother make jam tarts while her mother sits and drinks tea. It's tricky work, but Pearl enjoys it. She spoons a blob of scarlet jam into each tender pastry case, thinking about the girl with her smiley mouth and fascinating pants. Soon the tarts are put into the oven to bake and through the kitchen weaves a delicious, hot smell. Stand back, her granny says, as she gets the trays out. While the kettle boils and the table is laid, Pearl picks up a tart and rests her bottom lip on the scalding jam. Tears run from her eyes as she counts, then she screams. Two fat, translucent blisters are swelling on her lip. The women bump into each other to find ice and wet cloths, but neither one can stop her crying. Find out what she wants, Pearl's mother says, picking her up with difficulty and handing her over to her granny. Pearl points to the cabinet and the skating girl. You shall have it, my pet, her granny promises, you shall have it straight away. Pearl stretches out her hands, shuddering spasmodically, and waits for the cabinet to be opened.

Remembering

The branch Pearl sits on is like a settee. Far below her swinging feet, through the glowing, tender leaves, she can see endless bluebells. She sniffs hugely at the flowery cloud drifting up to her. She loves the bluebells' breath. Peering through delectable masses of foliage, she sees waves of colour so intense it must surely be purple. And here and there she can make out white crests of anemones drifting over the surface. Pearl lies back across her branch and looks up through the frilly leaves into the sky that's there, then not there, there, then not. White clouds snag in the thin hands of the tree. Everything is dazzling; blue, white, purple, green and back to blue. Pearl can't tell if she's smelling the blustery sky above or the swaying flowers far below. She would like to be a fierce bird, and go on strange journeys. Her beak would be scarlet, her talons silver, her black wings never tiring. No one knows that Pearl has stepped out of her life. No one knows where she is, or is looking for her. She examines the scars on her leg, and remembers drifting through the branches like a dandelion clock. Down I spiralled, soft and light. Down and down, she tells herself. But no, there was no spiralling, she thinks, and remembers careering through the branches, the thumping and crashing, how much it hurt. And then the sight of her bone, raw and private, after it ripped through the flesh. She remembers the undergrowth; how long it took for her father to find her. She remembers how happy she was, at first, lying there. Then she shrugs, and sinuously descends into her other life again.

No one

On the snowy way to church The Blob walks hand in hand between their parents, and Pearl sniffs freezing air until her nose burns, then blows out. She thinks the jets of nose-breath look like steam from an iron. Tell her to stop, her mother says to her father, who's been laughing at Pearl and her funny breathing. Against the morning's whiteness his strong black hair is brilliant. He puts his arm around Pearl's mother and just smiles. Pearl ignores the look her mother sends her. Daddy! she calls, and falls back into a plump snow hillock. Her mother darts over. Get up at once! she shouts, grasping Pearl's coat with mittened hands and yanking her into a standing position. What's wrong with you? she says, and shoves her. Walking ahead, the only sounds Pearl hears are the little hum her brother is making and the crump of feet in the snow. Everything has turned to monochrome, but the sky is a dull mauve. She eventually stops listening for her father to say something to her mother. Her cheeks are being slapped with sleet, and her feet feel dead. In church it's stifling. The smell of damp hair, floor wax and chrysan-themums make Pearl despair. With her fists she grinds her eyes, over and over again, until she sees explosions of stars and jagged bolts of blood. When she stops, the congrega-tion is a spiky crowd of ghosts who glare at her, clutching hymn books. Their mouths open and close as if they are gnashing their teeth. Though Pearl looks and looks, her own sweet bone girl is not to be seen. She tells herself that's to be expected; she would never come to a place like this.

Play time

Pearl has been playing a war game with the boys involving toy cars, planes, Lego and Action Men. Under the garden hedge she'd been practising sounds like engines revving and explosions until she was really good; she is the only girl allowed in the game. Pearl doesn't notice her cuts and bruises, or the rip in her shorts, until the game starts to wind down. The boys are impressed, she can tell. At midday, one by one, the boys are called for lunch, until only Pearl and Will are left, kneeling in the grass. They decide to go into the shed; they like pressing against each other in the dark. Today, the shed is half full of coal. It grates under the door as Will pulls it shut. The smell inside is old and oil-rich; they can taste coal dust. Will has wiry hands and Pearl feels them round her neck. She takes a pocket torch from the shelf and turns it on. A pale yellow glow lights Will's smudged face as he takes the torch. I want to look at you now, he says solemnly. Pearl pulls her shorts down to her knees and holds up her sun-top. The torch beam waves like a wand until it shines on her flat nipples and belly. Will puts his finger into her navel, then drops down to the neat split between her legs. He rubs his finger in and out. Pearl can't help laughing. Don't make a noise, Will says. He kneels to kiss her bruised knee and bleeding arm. Then it's Pearl's turn. She unzips Will and rummages with her hand until she finds his rooty little prick. The torch rests in the coals; along its splayed beam black lumps glint and flicker. I love you, Will says. In the sparkling dark Pearl kisses his mouth.

Favourites

Pearl and her brother are having a holiday with their grandmother. Her garden has winding, lavender-frilled paths and an orchard. Untended raspberry plants, weighed down with thumb-long, scarlet fruit, scrawl over beech hedges. Lettuces bolt, sending clouds of seeds adrift. Pearl loves creeping through undergrowth, curling up in the warm nests her granny's startled cats vacate when they hear her approach. She picks the almost white roses her grandmother prefers, and nibbles tiny tomatoes. They are allowed anywhere and can eat anything they want. Nobody calls them in. No one wants them to explain what they have been doing. Long afternoons go by when sunshine turns the greenhouse air to perfume, and the beds of shaggy purple dahlias droop. It's shaded near the pool, and Pearl and The Blob lie by the plant-spiked water, dazzled by the spangles of colour darting from the dragonflies who live between the trees and the pool's surface. One day, their granny brings them a big, tinkling jug of ice-cold lemonade and a plate of warm sausage rolls for lunch. Pearl lies with her head in the elastic hollow between her brother's ribs and hips. So, she says, her mouth full of crumbly pastry and delicious meat, who do you like best, Mother or Father? The dragonflies alight in unison on the tall, cerise flowers grouped about the pool. As they rise, wings whirring, and the flowers sway, her brother puts his grubby hand on Pearl's head. I like you best, he says. Pearl smiles at the drowsy garden. And I like Mother best, Pearl says. 'Course you do, her brother answers.

God

Pearl isn't afraid of God. The other kids in Junior Endeavour learn Scripture texts and practise Sword Drill with white Bibles, jumping up to answer questions. They can recite the books of the Bible backward, and always learn the verse of the week. Fee especially. The two of them walk through grassy evening air to the meeting, past the graveyard, amongst the trees where birds whistle so perfectly. Pearl dawdles until they reach the village. She's dragging one foot in the gutter. Fee has been showing her full reward book of Bible-scene stickers. You get a prize, she says. Pearl makes a bored face. But you should care about God, my love, Fee says. Why? Pearl asks. They look at Pearl's ruined shoe. He's dangerous, that's all, Fee says. They go into a side room of the chapel. Children gallop and shout. The smell of God is everywhere, and Pearl sniffs it. A boy collides with Fee, knocking her down. Pearl makes a note of who he is, but now she's got something to do. She slips through a door into the chapel. It's gloomy in the enormous space; silent but vibrating, as if an invisible thing with vast wings is hovering overhead. Pearl walks to the front pew. Before her a table rears up. On its tawny surface is an oversized bowl of cream roses, their faces open. Pearl takes a deep breath, cups her hands to her mouth and shouts out a terrible word. It feels as if the wings above have frozen mid-flight. Then she peers forwards. The rose stems start to quiver and, finally, one petal drops onto the burnished wood with the softest tap. Is that all? Pearl says, under her breath.

Overnight

Pearl's father tells her she has to go and stay with her cousin Mim for the night. Something is wrong with her mother again. Yes, Daddy, she says, and hugs him round the waist. But really, Pearl thinks, no one has to tell me, I know more than anyone in the world about my mother. I love you, Daddy, she says, and waits to hear him say my good girl. Then he unwinds her arms and is not there. Someone drives Pearl to her cousin's. From the back seat of the car she watches, but her father doesn't wave goodbye. Her aunt Betty has laid a place for her at the table, even though Pearl won't eat or speak. She keeps hold of her overnight bag and curls up behind a chair in the lounge, singing her two-note la-la, la-la, la-la song. Her aunty says, not to worry. I'm putting out a little plate of things you may like later. Her cousin Mim sits on the chair arm and plays with Pearl's hair until it's time to go upstairs, but Pearl refuses to meet her soft glance. They share a bed, and Pearl hugs and kisses Mim with concentration in the dark. She has rough skin behind her knees that sometimes cracks and bleeds, and Pearl likes to rub those places, but not tonight. So what else do you want to do? her cousin asks. Don't know yet, Pearl says. She listens to Mim breathing beside her, and wonders where The Blob is. One bright star trembles through a gap in the curtains and sends a beam of crystals straight into Pearl's head. She grips Mim between the legs, squeezing the mysterious, folded layers of skin there. Stop, she whispers furiously when Mim makes a noise. It has to be silent.

Berries

Will and Pearl are wading. As soon as the stream swells, flooding its own little beaches, drowning the tough, sparse grass on its margins, it's the thing they do. Each breath they take is like a snatch of invisible, moist cloud. And on these wet days, in the stream, there's always a moment when Pearl steps into an unknown pool and watches the water quiver at the rims of her wellingtons. She loves that wait, as the stream laps the thin rubber, before it tumbles down into her socks. She and Will stand and feel the water pour in. Now the air vibrates with rain, and the mint and submerged watercress shine; the marigolds glint with gems of liquid, and the stream's surface is wobbling and busy. Their feet are cold and delicious inside their boots. Droplets stand on the woollen filaments of their jumpers. Blackbirds sing worm-songs in the oak trees as Will asks Pearl if he can be her boyfriend. He grasps her warm hands and kisses them with his smiling mouth. Pearl sees that Will's eyes are the colour of the soaking sky, and his blond hair has darkened into curls. First things first, she says. They empty their boots and wring out their socks. Then Pearl leads him to a place she knows about, deeper in the woods. Every leaf and blade is glossy. She picks a handful of scarlet berries for him. Eat these, she says. Without a word he chews the berries to a creamy pulp and swallows them. Almost immediately he vomits. Pearl holds his forehead and rubs his bent back as he retches. Yes, Will, she says finally, for now I will be your girlfriend. Then she wipes his mouth with her hand.

Bird

Pearl and her brother are in the hedge, watching for their father to bring them chips and fishcakes wrapped in paper. At last Pearl sees his trousers with their brown shoes coming across the lawn. Here you are, he says, squatting down with a tray full of things for them to eat. Thanks, Daddy, they call out, and rip open the warm, clammy parcels. I know, Pearl says, we could be baby eagles. And that was our father eagle bringing us dinner. It's what father eagles do. This sounds good to The Blob, so they eat up, enjoying each hot, squashy chip as if it were a worm. These are mice, Pearl states, biting fiercely at a fishcake. What is this apple drink? her brother asks. Just apple drink, shtoopid, Pearl says. When they've finished they go indoors. Pearl peeps through the lounge door and sees her father sitting alone. Grabbing her brother's arm as he's about to run in, she whispers, stop! I'm thinking. Her father looks small somehow, and she doesn't like it. We'll be birds for Daddy, she tells her brother. But her brother is unsure. Watch me, she says, and glides into the room with The Blob trailing behind her. On the rug in front of her father she does a dance. Look, Daddy, she calls. I'm a greater spotted baby eagle! Their father opens his eyes. As her brother gets up onto the settee, Pearl flies and swoops, flies and calls, all over the room until she sees her father smile. Then she flutters down and curls herself at his feet. The Blob and her father laugh out loud, Pearl is so funny. I can do this any time you want, she cheeps, out of breath.

Falling down

Pearl has been sent to bed early. She listens to the children in the street, and the ice-cream van's tune, and the birds singing their evening songs to one another. She's decided to wait till everyone's asleep. Then she's going to the park. She thinks about the empty swings swaying from their chilly chains. And the trees, with their black trunks and millions of gently moving leaves, and all the snaking branches full of huddled birds. She sees herself treading the wet grass, climbing the steps of the tall slide. Maybe she'll sit in the cage at the top and look at everything. It doesn't seem long before the house is silent. Pearl looks through her curtains. The cones of light falling from the street lamps have changed from orange to lemon. She drifts through the front door and down the path. Then she's wandering into the park. The chestnut trees are shedding crinkled petals as she passes beneath them, and the perfume of the night plants makes her stop and breathe, over and over again. Then she sees her skeleton girl waiting on a swing, so she joins her. Even though she knows they shouldn't, they start to go higher than Pearl has ever swung before, laughing together. At the very highest point the skeleton girl loses her grip and falls from the swing with a swift, whooshing rattle. It's terrible, and Pearl leaps off. There on the ground is a scrabble of bones. Pearl quickly scoops them all into a carrier bag she finds lying nearby. Picking the skull up last, she holds it in both cupped hands and sobs, this is all my fault, I should be taking better care of you.

Bump

Honey tells Pearl about the baby she used to take out. I love babies, she says, making a thumb-sized mud child and giving it to Pearl. You can do stuff with them, and they can't tell anyone. Pearl crushes the friable brown baby between her palms. Apart from with The Blob, she hadn't thought of that before. Honey puts lumps of mud on each of Pearl's toes, then flattens them out to cover her nails. Pearl shapes a huge, hanging mud nose and fits it on Honey. They stare at each other in the hedge gloom. Honey's wide smile looks odd curving out behind her rough, earth nose. We have a baby in our street, Pearl says, so they clean up and knock on the baby's door. The baby's mother is a friend of Pearl's family. Keep to the paths, she says, tucking a blanket in. We promise, they say. Inside the buggy the pink baby is propped up on a frilly pillow. Pearl and Honey take turns to push. Soon they come to a stile in the hedge. I know, says Pearl, we could easily get this thing over. They manage to lift the buggy up to the top bar of the stile. I'm puffed, Honey says, and sits down. Pearl thinks she can do it alone, but suddenly everything upends. The baby flies out and lands in some nettles like a knot of washing. The trees lean in and a bird trills while they stand, transfixed. Then Pearl vaults the stile, pulls the baby up by her talcy shawls and plonks her back in the righted pushchair. The baby is quivering; about to yell, covered in scarlet nettle stings and dead leaves. Its soiled bonnet is askew. Pearl and Honey hold hands; worst of all, there is a greeny-grey lump growing above the baby's right eye.

The rules

Earlier, Fee turned pale and sobbed as Pearl told her she couldn't go with the gang. It's because of Honey, isn't it? Fee asked. You like her best now. Pearl looked at Fee's sweet eyes and sticky-out teeth. You won't keep up, that's all, she said, scrambling out of the hedge. Pearl's impatient to be gone. She's been kept in for two weeks, and cloud-boats are skimming along the endless sky; there are birds darting like arrows across its surface. The gang walks up through the houses until they reach a lane. This is where the mountain starts to grow. They are making for a secret way through the ferns called The Slippery Path. Eventually they stand on its steep, shaggy surface. Branched ferns tall as people tower on either side. They plunge in and battle through until they find a suitable space. Fern stalks squeak as the gang take off all their clothes. Pearl tells each one to stand up in turn. No one is allowed to move. She whacks them with a long stalk on their bottoms and bellies. She smacks Will harder than the rest. Then she tells him to wee. The sound of splashing makes them all smile. Good, Pearl tells him, her face flushed, now everybody eat. The gang swap sandwiches and drink warm squash, eating quietly. The air is humming drowsily with insects, and they find a slow-worm. Leave it alone, Pearl commands, standing up, naked but for her sandals. She swishes her stalk just above the gang's heads, and looks at each of them in turn. Right, you lot, now it's time for a special game, she says. It's called Kiss, Kick, or Torture. And I will explain the rules.

Cut

Pearl only has to look at her front door to know how it will be inside. The oval window above the letterbox changes colour. Like an eye that's sometimes vacant, sometimes terrified, sometimes blind with rage, the bluey-green glass subtly alters. It's a language Pearl can understand. Once or twice even the brass door handle has told her things. Today, standing at the gate, she notices the colours in the window are almost bleached out. The garden path stretches for miles before her. When she eventually reaches the porch and touches the door handle, it is so cold her skin melds to it for a second. Pearl pushes the door wide and leaps in, calling for her brother. She feels the air pulsing with a sort of static. In the kitchen, she sees him standing alone. She drops her bag and goes to him. Splayed on the table are her mother's huge black-and-silver scissors. The Blob is silent, but from his eyes tears drop steadily. What's happened? Pearl asks, her voice businesslike. She can see soft mounds of chestnut curls all around him on the floor. His scalp shows through, pink and raw in places. Pearl starts to shake. She strokes his bristly head and sees his ear is bleeding. The neckline of his jumper is ragged and chopped at. Pearl walks to the sink and turns on the tap. Sit down now, she says to her brother. I'll clean you up. He stiffly folds himself onto a chair, hardly blinking. I'll say I did it, he states. Promise you won't tell. She tries to answer, but her mouth won't work. Quickly she locks the back door; through the window she can see her mother running towards the house. You're next, Pearly! she's shouting.

All better

Pearl strides out, counting the steps it takes to get away from the house. Soon they are at the canal. This is a good idea, my love, Fee says, linking arms. They arrive at a stretch of brambles twice their height. The sun hits the bushes each afternoon, so it's studded with hundreds of glossy black fruit. Orange butterflies rest on the topmost branches. Beneath, spears of cuckoo pint are unfurling in the shade. Inside each tender sheath Pearl can see a column of jade-green berries ripening. Don't touch those, she says. When Fee finds a nice blackberry she calls, look at this beauty! and Pearl pulls the thorny stems down for her. The way Fee darts about is calming. Even when she scratches her arm, she still smiles her crooked smile. Let me look, Pearl says, examining the red-dotted weal on the inside of Fee's freckled arm. As she sucks the broken skin she hears Fee's snatched intake of breath. Pearl straightens, and, turning slowly, she sees a man on the other side of the path; she's not sure how long he's been there. He's mouthing strange words at them. What do you want? Pearl asks, shielding Fee. From the mess of his grey trousers the man fishes out his erect, sore-looking penis and steps nearer, thrusting with his hips so that its wet, stretched tip bobs from side to side. Pearl watches for a few seconds, then she starts to purse her lips. Really? she thinks, raising her eyebrows. Her unimpressed gaze acts like a pinprick on a red balloon, and his penis shrivels. He covers it with his coat and shuffles away. It's okay now, Fee, Pearl says, hugging her. I've made it all better.

Beans

Even though Honey's parents have forbidden them from seeing each other, she and Pearl walk home together in the rain after school. No more babies for us, Honey says. Maybe, says Pearl, tilting her mouth to the fat drops falling from the trees. They begin to imagine a delicious meal waits for them. What will you really be eating? Honey asks. It's stew night, Pearl says. I'd love to stuff a bowl of stew, Honey says. I doubt that, Pearl says, and thinks about the parsnips she always mistakes for potatoes, the thready meat and swede nubs she retches over. If I could just have bread and gravy, she says, I'd be a happy girl. Why don't you, then? Honey asks, taking her hand. Pearl thinks about stew fumes in the kitchen, and her tight-lipped mother dishing out. She looks at Honey with her glossy hair and pink nails and realises she has no idea about stew, or fish and parsley sauce, or liver and onions. Want to come to mine? Honey asks. Dropping their wet things in the hall, they go to the kitchen. Honey opens a cupboard full of crisps and biscuits. Help yourself, she says. Pearl gazes and gazes at the lovely treats. No, she says. Ice-cream then? Honey offers. But Pearl is silent. I know, Honey says, waffles and syrup. Not for me, Pearl says. I'd better go. But still she stays, watching as Honey opens a tin of baked beans. They're delish cold, she tells Pearl, offering her a spoonful. Astonished, Pearl opens her mouth, takes the beans and runs out into the rain without her coat. The beans are savoury and sweet. To Pearl they taste like food from another country.

Mer-children

Pearl and her brother are in the bath. He's at the tap end. She squeezes a sponge and says that, really, she's too old to share a bath with him. I know, he says as he busily soaps her feet. Now can I play? Pearl sighs and closes her eyes, so he starts talking to her toes. He likes to pretend they are his children. Wriggle them, he says. You have to wriggle. It's warm in the bathroom, and her brother's echoey whisper soothes Pearl. She imagines the damp bathroom whirling through space, past the streaking stars, little puffs of steam solidifying as they're pulled through the window's opening. But it feels too lonely out there, and Pearl opens her eyes. She keeps wriggling with one foot, and plants the other on her brother's chest. He looks like a mer-boy with his sprouting tendrils of new hair and wet eyelashes. Through her foot she can feel his steady heartbeat. If you like, she says, you can lean on me. So he turns around and rests between her legs, his back against her stomach. Their brown knees break through the milky water. Shall we play being mer-people? Pearl asks, her mouth against his soapy hair. Imagine; we could swim and swim and explore the whole ocean if we liked. We could dive into caves and see all the beautiful sea-creatures stuck to the walls. What would we eat, though? her brother asks; fish is horrible. No problem, she says. We'll feed on delicious plants. She can tell he's thinking. Will our parents be there? he says. No, Pearl answers. Mer-children don't have anybody, just each other. Okay then, he says, and starts to make elaborate swimming gestures.

Dreams

There are some nights when Pearl lies in her bed, serious as a small effigy, while outside, creatures with gills like open wounds and wings ragged as winter cabbage leaves gather at the garden gate. There is no one to look after her; she is perfectly alone in the world. In the dark street, the lamp posts writhe with gleaming white serpents. All sorts of eyes are focused on the open window of Pearl's room. For hours she hears halloos and snickering, her name being called by voices trying to sound friendly, nails screeching against the flimsy front door. She knows that in two bounds the stairs could be breached. In her small room Pearl's naked, unwashed foot is hanging over the side of the bed, inches above the pongy, bone-strewn lair of a wet-skinned animal who is waking up, feeling famished, testing his jaws. And here's Pearl's delicious, swinging foot, dangling like a pasty at a picnic. She's determined not to hide it; this is some sort of test, after all. She slits her eyes and sees a shape woven through the slatted headboard of her bed. It leans out and watches Pearl unkindly, dribbling on the pillow. Hot breath paws her cheeks, but she keeps her chest still, still, still. Finally the thing sighs and undulates away. Then, like a needle of silver thread piercing the neck of an old black dress, a bird shouts three radiant phrases. The stars faint, the sky blinks and Pearl stretches, throwing off the night, wanting a glass of milk and a breakfast of bacon and eggs. All the creatures rear up, appalled, and gallop away on soft, heavy hooves, or dissolve in spurts of moisture.

Clearing up

Like a cold white hand held up to Pearl's face, her mother's bedroom door remains closed. The Blob has been taken away, and strange people are in the house when she gets home from school. Usually, Pearl grabs something to eat, edging round whoever's in the kitchen, and runs out again. No one tries to stop her, or asks where she's going. Sometimes she hides in the airing cupboard and chews energetically. Am I invisible? she asks herself; no one seems to see her these days. Often she has no clean socks or pants to wear. Once she crept into her mother's room. It smelt sickening. Pearl stood by the bed and looked down. Finally, her mother's eyes opened and she whimpered, who are you? Pearl could see crusty deposits around her lips. It looked as if someone had chopped off all her creamy hair. She sank into the bed when Pearl loomed over her. You won't hurt me, will you? she asked. Pearl felt herself growing huge, filling the small, warm room. She bent over her mother and whispered, you'll just have to wait and see. Screams followed her as she slipped quietly out. Most evenings Pearl hovers in the gloomy lounge. One night she unravels her mother's knitting and burns it. Another time she gathers all the stupid pieces of bric-a-brac and smashes them behind the shed, scrabbling at the dank, wormy earth to cover the sharp bits. Late in the evening her father will come down, and Pearl can rest her head on his shoulder and stroke his hands. He doesn't seem to notice that, gradually, she is removing all traces of her mother.

Now what?

Pearl walks home from school a new way, thinking about her house, how it feels like an empty, two-storey fridge. She's thinking so hard she bumps into a girl who has been standing, arms crossed, in the middle of the path. This girl is taller than Pearl, with a red mouth and black, stringy plaits. Fight? she asks, punching Pearl's chest. Immediately, Pearl swings her school bag with such conviction at the girl's head that the girl falls sideways, twisting her leg. Then they struggle. Pearl has to work hard, but she finally pins the girl to the ground. Now what? Pearl asks, trying not to pant while she straightens her clothes. The girl's leg is bleeding and one plait has been pulled into a messy bundle. Why are you hanging round here, anyway? the girl asks, scrambling to her feet. Pearl doesn't answer. Come on home with me, the girl says. Her name is Nita. It's fuggy inside the house, and Pearl can smell fish, burning coal and cigarette smoke. I like your house, she tells Nita. In the lounge Pearl sits alone next to a sleeping dog. A tall boy slides in through the partially open door. He's carrying a short bamboo stick, which he swishes about. Pearl notices he has one overlarge, staring eye. Why don't you look at me? he asks. Am I too ugly for you? Yes, Pearl answers. He tells her to stand up. Okay, she says. The boy uses his stick to lift Pearl's skirt up. Then he jabs it into her crotch. Pearl eyes him coolly. Now what? she says. He hears Nita coming so he deftly uses the stick to rearrange Pearl's clothes. Gotta go, Pearl says. Will you come again? Nita asks. You bet, Pearl tells her.

Ever ready

Since he's come home, her brother seems smaller, more tearful, trailing after Pearl with his tiger under his arm. She gets angry, seeing him this way. Come here, she calls in their dark room. He dashes across to her bed. Under the covers, cross-legged, Pearl sits up and makes a space for him to nestle. He curves his body around her. Where's your tiger? she asks, turning on her pocket torch and shining it on him. The Blob pulls the tiger out from inside his pyjama top. Give, Pearl says, and holds out her hand. The tiger's eyes have gone, and his mouth is unravelling. Pearl gently smushes him into her brother's face. You know he's disabled, don't you? she says. The Blob looks as if he's going to cry. I'll sew some new buttons on, she tells him. Now stop dripping and say what story you'd like. Soon Pearl is telling him about nasty aliens. How they lean out over the tops of the craters they live in and look down. They plan to zoom earthward on moonbeams, and suck children up through their long, alien noses. Why? her brother asks. Food, of course, Pearl says, and goes on describing how, maybe, at this very moment, the million-eyed aliens are hungrily gazing down at them. The Blob puts his hands over his ears. Pearl can see how their little wigwam, aglow with torchlight, would shine out into space. Let them come, she states, holding up her torch to show him the words on it. Her curl is standing out like a crescent moon and her eyes glitter. Watching Pearl, her brother hugs his tiger and smiles. Ever Ready, she tells him, thumbing her chest. That's me.

Winner

In the garden, Pearl and The Blob are having one of their periodic competitions. I'll choose a challenge, Pearl says, and we'll see who's the best. Her brother is listening as he lies in the tussocky grass under the apple trees, playing with his white guinea pig. Pearl stands over him. You're not scared, are you? she says. There's always hope, you know. Then she nudges him briskly with her foot until he gets up. He disappears behind the shed to the hutch. In you go, Dave, she hears him say. I'll bring you a treat later. Yeah, Dave, she calls, you keep out of this. You might get your fur dirty. The Blob nods as Pearl explains that they both have to climb the tallest apple tree and jump down onto the sloping edge of the old wall. Me first, she says, scrambling up the knotted trunk. The branches are covered with a crumbly, bitter-smelling lichen that sticks to her palms. Pearl sees tight bunches of apples pocked with fungus as she goes higher. Some of the branches give way under her feet. There's a place where a gap appears through the foliage, and far below she can just make out the top of the wall. Pearl launches off and flies through the leaves, landing like someone balancing on a surfboard. Then she jumps to the ground and her brother is on his way up. She's startled by how fast he's climbing these days. He shouts wildly, crashing through the branches. Then there is the sound of collapsing stones and muffled screaming. Pearl rushes over. Her brother is gasping, flat on the grass, his forehead wet with blood, his leg partially covered by stones. Pearl surveys him, hands on hips. I win, she says.

Choke

In the lounge The Blob sits at their mother's feet while she feeds him dripping chunks from a huge orange. The evening light is shot through with bursts of zest. Saliva drenches Pearl's mouth, but she hugs her knees in a corner of the settee, unable to shake off the feeling that something is going to happen. Each time she checks, the two of them seem happy enough, chomping their orange, so Pearl closes her eyes and decides to count; maybe her father will come home before she has even got to fifty. Suddenly there's a noise that doesn't sound right. Pearl sees her mother stuffing pieces of orange into her brother's mouth, steadying his struggling head with her free hand. For a moment Pearl can't move. Her mother drops both hands and watches, fascinated, as The Blob's face turns scarlet and his lips swell. Pearl knows he is struggling to breathe. Do something, Mother, she manages to say. But her mother does nothing. Her brother's grunts are the only sounds in the room. He collapses onto his hands and knees while her mother, still transfixed, says tonelessly, no Pearl, you should do something. Suddenly, Pearl feels her muscles release. She dashes across the lounge and shoves her finger and thumb into his throat, pulling out a lumpy membrane of semi-chewed orange. The Blob sits up, sobbing, and Pearl makes her way unsteadily back to the settee. They both stare at their mother. Her lap is full of curves of peel. Well, she says, gathering them up in her apron, I can't just sit here, I have things to do. Then she leaves the room.

Sick

The gang are bored. Pearl watches Chris and Steven list-lessly punch each other on the arms, then calls Honey over and whispers briefly into her thick hair. Dragging the boys apart, she shouts, attention you lot, follow me. Hon's parents are out, so we're going there. By the front door she tells Fee and the boys to wait. In the kitchen she and Honey fill bowls with all sorts of food from the fridge and cupboards. Some things they defrost in boiling water. Shoes off! she tells the gang, before leading them into the kitchen. I will choose two items of food for each of you, she explains, you have to eat them without throwing up. They all think this is a great idea, and start boasting to each other about how they are never, ever sick. Order! shouts Pearl, and selects Fee first. Seriously, she chooses a blob of corned beef and a teaspoon of cough medicine as the gang watch. Fee sniffs the spoon and starts to whine, her big front teeth winking. Pearl shovels in the spoon. Fee runs to the sink, retching, while everybody laughs. Not bad, Pearl says. Next! Not one of the gang can stop themselves being sick. Honey manages to chew hers the longest. Will refuses. Honestly! Pearl says, tapping him on the head. Now me. You can each choose one thing. Soon the big spoon is towering with, among other things, a soft sprout, peanut butter, a slick of Vick's rub, a prune and a crumbled stock cube. Give, Pearl com-mands, and pushes the whole lot in. Tears fly from her eyes while she chews vigorously. Then, tipping her head back, she swallows. The gang let out a sigh. Awesome, Will says, speaking for everybody.

Perky

Nita pulls the key on its string through the letterbox and opens the door. So, who's stick boy? Pearl asks, and sniffs, checking that the house smells the same. Nita makes a face. My brother, she says. The big dog who'd slept beside her on her first visit trots up and lifts his front paws onto Pearl's chest. Usually he bites people, Nita says. Don't you, Perks? Pearl ruffles his ears. I don't believe it, she says. His shaggy legs flump as they hit the carpet. Through the kitchen window the garden looks as if it's been ploughed. A TV lies in the mud, and there's a deflated paddling pool with brown water in its folds amongst a stand of nettles. Pearl sees Nita's brother, so she goes out. The name's Ken, he says, slashing weeds with his stick. He looks Pearl up and down. Big girl in some areas, aren't you? he says. Even I can see that. Pearl gazes at him. He's about seventeen, and his face is odd. Finally she clocks he has a false eye. He flourishes his stick, then uses it to circle her breasts. Stepping behind her, he smacks her buttocks with it. Pearl stands still. Well, you're a little toughie, he says, facing her again. He slips his stick under his arm. Pearl is silent. His smile fades. Do you want to hold my eye? he asks. Putting one hand over the socket, he performs a scooping movement with the index finger of the other hand. Pearl is ready. He plops the moist, oval eye onto her open palm. Backing away, she feels how warm and heavy it is. Oi! Give it back! he shouts, his empty lid like a sad little mouth. The dog is sniffing around the bins. Fetch, Perky! Pearl calls, lobbing the eye into the ruined paddling pool.

Wind chime

Pearl wishes her father would read to her like he did when she was little. You can read to yourself now. My little girl is far too old for that sort of thing, he'd said from behind his newspaper when she asked him to come up after she was in bed. In her room Pearl slowly takes her clothes off, not caring if she wakes her brother, and drops each item one by one. Nothing is the same, she thinks, remembering her father's deep voice flooding over her as she used to lie all safe under the covers. She tries to make herself cry, but no tears will come. From the shelf she takes down the book her father liked most, and lays it, flopped open, on the floor. Then with bare feet she stands on the spine, listening for the tiny breaking snaps. As she picks the book up, pages flutter loose and zigzag to the carpet. Oh no, Pearl says quietly, and gathers them up. Then she lays everything out on the bed and puts each page in order. She spends a long time trying to Sellotape the pages back into the book, but now it's unstable, scruffy, useless. As she struggles with the reel of sticky tape she starts to cry. At last she lies on the bed and allows the ruined book to fall to the floor, using a forearm bristling with torn-off segments of tape to wipe her wet face. Once her eyes are clear she looks around and notices her skeleton girl hanging from the hook on the bedroom door. She's trying to make Pearl laugh by shaking herself about. Pearl can't help smiling slightly; the clattering sound is almost like a cute little wind chime. But even so, there is no sound of footsteps climbing the stairs.

Not any more

At last, The Blob has been given a bedroom of his own. Pearl has their old, shared room. She should be the one to have a new room. It's only right. But then, she thinks, does it really matter? The room feels new, now all his rubbishy boy-things are gone, and Pearl's private bits and pieces are on the windowsill; just her clothes and shoes are in the wardrobe, just her dressing gown hangs on the back of the door. And she won't have to listen to his weird, stop-start breathing. Now she can do certain things she couldn't do before, when he was in her face all the time. On the first night they are left alone, she and The Blob go to their rooms and shut their doors. It seems important to celebrate, so Pearl decides to dance for a while, and is dizzy when she finally gets into her nightie, turns on the bedside lamp and settles with a book. She wonders what he's doing, all alone. Eventually there's a knock. Really? thinks Pearl, and smiles. She listens until he knocks again. Get lost, she shouts, and sits up. The door swings open and she sees her brother standing, a fuzzy glow emanating from his silhouette. He is naked, and his penis is thick and long. He stares at her and she stares back. He waits with his hands on his bony hips, swaying so that his penis looks as if it's shaking its head. Pearl picks up her book and thinks about the man on the canal bank, and how the red tip of his penis emerged from his filthy trousers. Well? her brother says. Sighing, Pearl starts to read. Well, she answers. You're certainly not The Blob any more, are you?

Bleeding

On Friday afternoon there is a special class. This is s'posed to give you all the info you need, you know, to be an adult, Honey tells Pearl as they sprawl on their back-row chairs. Pearl thinks that's stupid. Prepare to be sick, Honey says, making retching sounds. It's periods today. Pearl sits electrified throughout the class. Blood? she thinks, really? It's disgusting. The boys snigger, shifting in their seats. Stop being so childish! the teacher shouts. But, Pearl thinks, just what's wrong with being a child? On the way home from school she's unable to speak. Honey is trying to guess who's started their period and who hasn't. Have you, Pearl? she asks. 'Course, Pearl says shortly. Then she runs, feeling as if someone is trying to grab her by the hair. At home she can't eat any food. Please yourself, her mother tells her, and turns back to the oven. Don't think there'll be any snacks later, madam. Pearl goes to her room, closes her curtains and lies down. So, soon she'll be bleeding every month. It's hard to take in. How can that be right? she wonders. A person only bleeds when they've cut themselves. And it's hard enough, say, bleeding from your arm. She thinks of all the women and girls she knows. At any time, any number of them might be bleeding into their pants. It's so gross she can't stand it. Then she thinks about her mother. The idea of her mother oozing blood from between her legs makes Pearl feel faint. She dashes to the bathroom and throws up in the toilet. Wiping her mouth with her hand, she catches her breath; her father must know about this. How does he feel?

Wall

In the gym Pearl and Fee hide in the sweaty little room that holds the vault horse and rubber mats. Squashed in a corner between the wall and a bin of weights, they share a chocolate bar. The point is, says Fee, calmly sucking, adults are so deadly dull. I don't know why, they just are. Pearl can't be bothered to respond; even talking about it is boring. But after a short silence she says, no, it's mothers who're the worst, and pushing four squares of chocolate in Fee's mouth, she says she can tell why. It was in her dream. Okay, says Fee, tell on, my love. Pearl describes a wide, green, flat valley. And rearing up halfway across it, a smooth wall the height of two houses that thousands of mothers are trying to climb over. Crowds are fighting to get near the wall. Some are disappearing over the top all along its length, skirts over their heads, high heels shooting off in all directions. Frantic women fall back and trample those below, while ragged vultures scream and swoop at them. Pearl has climbed to the top of the wall and peered down, and only she knows that over there is a huge, lonely desert, full of white bones; hundreds of miles of bones, stretching from the foot of the enormous wall out to the hills. The scouring wind rushing up and over the wall scraped a vile dust over Pearl's face, coating her lips as she looked. And all around her, mothers were falling headlong, never to be seen again. Didn't you try and warn them? Fee asks. Totally no point, Pearl says, and gets up, brushing herself off. You know mothers.

Change

Pearl is thirteen now, and she thinks things will surely be different. The day after her birthday she wakes up in her usual position and the usual curtains are hanging at her usual windows. Everything is nauseatingly the same. Finally, she throws back the covers, lifts her nightdress up to her chin and stretches out in the bed. It's as if the room is filled with twinkling fireworks. She was right, after all. Overnight, she has transformed. In just eleven hours her breasts are different; the hard lumps at their centres have softened, expanded, filling out each pillowy globe. Her fawn-coloured nipples sit like two beautiful kisses in exactly the right position. She stands at the mirror and takes off her boring nightdress. Her waist has contracted, and the shape of her hips is stunning. Her legs are longer. There's her head, just the same, but the body below is new. Pearl's heart is whacking against her ribs. She feels as if she'll burst, or float, or explode, it's all so great. She dresses and drifts downstairs. Her family are at the breakfast table. No one looks when she comes in. Her brother hoovers up cereal, her mother absently sips coffee and her father is snatching mouthfuls of toast as he reads the paper. Pearl waits to see what will happen. Eat, her mother says, and stretches her lips back to her cup. Pearl climbs onto a chair and stands, hands on hips. Daddy? she says, see? But her father looks up briefly, and then falls on his toast again. Pearl stamps her foot and shouts, Are you blind, or something? Then she jumps lightly down, and leaves them all gaping.

Work it out

Pearl is in the highest nook of her beech tree, but something doesn't feel right. Maybe she will lose her balance and fall. She knows she won't, though: there is no wind, and the trunk is solid under her palms. It's my head, she thinks. My head is weird, and she shakes her hair out to clear it. Nothing works. So she sits and tunes into the feeling. Then she shivers. Heavy insects are lumbering over her scalp. She lets go of the tree and starts to rub her head with both hands, even though her scalp is its usual smooth self. Now she feels a damp tongue of heat licking upwards from her chest to her face. Deep inside her body a fist is dragging everything down. Pearl clutches the trunk of the tree. This must be what it feels like to faint, she thinks. The insects on her scalp skitter and her eyelids droop. Then a leaf-sweet breeze runs a refreshing hand over her neck and cheeks. It seems to blow the insects out of her hair, and Pearl is able to climb down. She lies flat and places trembling hands on her hip bones. All around, the air is green. Down inside, something is grinding slowly, and it hurts. What's happening to me? Pearl thinks. Her new breasts are burning, and saliva gushes into her mouth. Without any effort she is sick, neatly, onto the grass. Somehow, she gets home, pushing through the ferns and red campion. Mother, look! she calls, falling through the front door. Her mother half turns from the window. They both watch as a thin rope of blood runs down Pearl's leg. What shall I do now? she asks. Work it out for yourself, her mother says, turning back to the window.

Full

Pearl and her brother are playing draughts in the garden shed. Their father's jars of screws, his oiled tools and work gloves are all in the usual places. I'm so hungry, The Blob says, I can't concentrate on thrashing you. Oh really? Pearl says. That's a new one. She gets up from the floor. Won't be a mo, she tells him. I'll see what I can find. At the shed door she turns and adds, touch the pieces and you're a dead boy. Pearl slips up the unlit path into the kitchen and begins searching through the cupboards. Then she hears noises from upstairs and quickly grabs what she can. Soon, she and her brother are crunching their way through a jar of pickled onions. And for afters, she announces, holding up a block of orange jelly, we have this. Actually, we're quite privileged, she tells him, being allowed to eat anything we want. Silently they pull the stretchy, sticky cubes of jelly apart, each think-ing what they would really like to eat tonight. Pearl wins every round of draughts easily. How does it feel, you know, being defeated over and over again? she asks. Her brother leans back and puts the last jelly cube in his mouth. It's no problem, he says, smiling. I never mind you beating me, Pearl. Finally it's time to go to bed, and they both creep up the stairs. Don't forget to wash, you disgusting little twit, Pearl says. On the landing they bump into their father. Oh, you two, he says vaguely, rubbing his forehead. You must be hungry. Pearl puts her hand on her brother's shoulder and squeezes. No thanks, Daddy, she says. We're absolutely full. And she reaches to kiss him goodnight.

Easy

Pearl and Honey meet up under the hedge as a shower falls. Now they're bigger, it's a tight squeeze, but it's dry inside, and they watch as raindrops punch puddles into the lawn. They sit facing each other, cross-legged, and breathe in the yeasty, soaking earth of the garden. As rain falls on the baked concrete path, it gives up a smell that always reminds Pearl of the school holidays. I have a plan, she tells Honey. The next day Honey rounds up all the boys in the street. She makes them wait outside the old brick shed behind the garages. She's strict, and wants to know how much money they've each got. Next to some bushes covered with puffy white berries, she sorts the boys into line. Shut it! she shouts at the smallest one. And wipe your nose. Will stands apart, arms folded. Finally Pearl calls from the shed and the first boy gives his coins to Honey, shouldering his way in. The others shuffle, watching the closed door. Then in they go and out they stumble, looking stupefied, until it's Will's turn. Inside he can just make out Pearl tucking in her top as she lounges on a chair. He sits on her lap and puts an arm around her. She rests her head back and tells him he doesn't have to pay, but he says it's only fair. He kisses Pearl's forehead just where her hair flips up, and feels her hands with his, touching her palms, pushing his fingers between hers. Then he has to go home. Pearl and Honey walk to the sweet shop. Later, under the hedge, surrounded by chocolate toffee and sherbet fountains, Pearl stops mid-chew. It's amazing, she says, how no one's thought of doing this before.

Surprise

Pearl, Honey and Fee are in the park. It's evening and they should all be going home. They sit on the swings and watch little bats flitter about like black scraps under the trees' scribbled canopy. They look happy, Pearl says. I love bats. The other two make shuddering noises. In the dusk, Pearl smiles as they talk about the things they hate. Periods, mind, says Fee. Re-volt-ing. Oh yuck, agrees Honey. Then she gets off her swing and shows them the little zip-up purse her mother has given her. Inside are pads and wipes. Fee starts to jerk her swing higher. Me wants a cute, periody purse too! she gasps, her thin red hair floating. Bloody periods! Honey shouts into the empty park as she twirls around. Pearl's hands grasp the chains as she leans back from her swing; her head is to the ground and her legs up in the air. Her eyes search the mole-grey sky for the first evening star while she thinks about how she has to hide all her used pads in her cupboard. How she loathes the way they smell and stiffen. Gotta run, girlies, she says suddenly. At home, before she goes to find her mother's handbag, Pearl peeps into the bathroom and looks at her mother's rounded, semi-submerged legs spread apart in the bath. Safe in her room she sits on her bed and examines the conker-shiny leather bag with its white stitching and pointed corners. She has to use two hands to click open the tight clasp. Then Pearl empties her musky heap of stuck-together, soiled pads into its depths, snaps the clasp shut and quickly puts it back where she found it. Work this out for yourself, Mother, she thinks.

Out

Pearl and her father are going on their December visit to relatives. They have to catch two buses to reach the little village where her father was brought up. Pearl counts all the sparkling Christmas trees in the silvery-dim front room windows they pass. Every year she loses count. It doesn't matter; she leans against her father's rough overcoat, feeling his arm and leg against hers, and watches endless snow slanting outside the bus. At intervals her father passes her a tiny oblong of gum, and they chew together. Every year they go to the same houses, in the same order. At the first house, they are welcomed into an unbearably cosy, cramped hall, and as Pearl takes off her coat and mittens, an old lady exclaims how tall she's become, how grown-up she looks. Then they sit by the fire while slowly the kettle boils. Pearl carries a teapot and plates of cake in from the freezing kitchen. Wakey, wakey, says the old lady and scoops up a drooping cat. Conversation putters on while Pearl holds her teacup in both hands and stares into the fire, the iced cake on her plate neglected. Soon it's time to go. The old lady wraps the cake up for her. Outside, night is filling the streets, and windows shine yellowly as Pearl and her father walk up the silent hill, she with her arm through his, the snow wavering against their bulky coats. They almost bump into a woman laden with bags, who recognises her father and stops to talk. Pearl stands quietly, holding his hand. She studies his face, listening to the way he laughs gently when the woman asks him, and is this your wife?

Better

Pearl decides to study her mother's every move when her father's away. Each night she sits in bed, her nightdress done up to the neck, and makes notes in a book she was given as a birthday gift. Using her new fountain pen, and doing her best writing, she creates headings. Each subject gets a new page. Carefully she watches as the days unfold. Some things are simple; cooking, say, or cleaning. Others are so boring she doesn't bother to write them down. Her ideas on ways to do things more easily, or quickly, or better, are garlanded with flowers. There is a special section for her thoughts on lovely things to do, points she feels would make the house so much nicer to live in. And the biggest, most important thing doesn't need to be written down at all. Pearl knows that until the big thing is sorted out, nothing is possible. She has another, invisible list inside her head about that, and every day she tries to find something, no matter how small, to tick off it. Her mother begins to notice that she's being watched. Go away, she says at first, when Pearl appears from behind a door as she's preparing a meal, or knitting, or standing at the lounge window, or biting the skin around her scarlet nails. After a few days she starts to cry if she sees Pearl observing her. Finally, she loses her temper and screams until she exhausts herself. Why are you looking at me? she yells, while Pearl steadily stares her down. Go away, please, she wails. After a few weeks, Pearl has enough material. She reads right through the notebook, ticking as she goes. Sitting up in bed, she shuts the book. Yes, I can do all these things just as well, she thinks. If not ten times better.

Understandable

Pearl sits in front of Nita's huge TV with Perky beside her. How come you always have tins of Quality Street? she asks. My brother gets them, Nita says, settling herself on the rug, her mouth full of chocolate. Ken goes out now when Pearl appears. I don't know what you did to him, Nita says. But thanks. Poor Ken, Pearl thinks. He's right not to hang around. Nita can't believe Pearl's family don't have a telly. What do you do all evening? she asks. Pearl doesn't have an answer. She's mesmerised by the TV screen. The swollen face and wobbling mouth of a woman who's being strangled gives her a weird feeling, but she likes it. The chocolate melting in her mouth is somehow mixed up with it all. Turn this off, she says. It's stupid. Nita changes channels. Pearl rests her head on Perky's rough flank and thinks about her own lounge with its stiff chairs and empty fireplace. And, always on the coffee table, her mother's stupid, spiky work basket. When she gets home she's surprised to see her father pacing the hall. Are you waiting for me, Daddy? she asks. Then she stops. He is angry. What have I done wrong? she says, shocked. This is horrible, Pearl, he shouts, holding up her mother's handbag. I do not ever want to see disgusting female things like this again! Do you hear me? Then he slams the lounge door behind him. Pearl feels as if someone has raked out her insides. Her father has never before shouted at her like that. She sinks to the floor in the lonely, tiled hall and feels the thousands of seconds race up and over her body. Poor Daddy, she decides, after thinking until her legs are numb. Yes, it's understandable he should feel this way.

Opportunity

Pearl's grandmother gives her a rickety desk for her room. Pearl's been busy, putting her books on a shelf above it. She loves to sit at her desk and write stuff. The desk has drawers, and what's really good is they're lockable. In one of the drawers she puts all the little messages she's written to herself. Pearl's room is damp. In the wardrobe, her clothes sometimes grow mould. In winter they clump together. Her shoes bloom with grey powder if she doesn't wear them for a while. Black specks appear at the back of the wardrobe after it's rained. None of this bothers Pearl; she thinks her room smells like a mysterious dungeon. Now, after everything is sorted out, she takes a limp book down from her shelf and starts to flick through it. The wavy pages give off a mushroomy smell. Her eyes begin to water and she drops the book to rub them with both hands. Once she's started she can't stop. Her eyes burn and she grinds both knuckles into her sockets. Tears sting her cheeks. Her nose is blocked and she feels odd. She gets up and looks in the mirror at her wet face until she hears her father come through the front door. She practises a few sobs, then dashes downstairs and stumbles into the kitchen. Her mother and father are facing each other. What's happened? he asks, turning. Has someone upset you? Pearl runs and presses her cheek into his chest. He puts his arms around her heaving shoulders. Have you said something? he asks her mother. Pearl keeps sobbing, but she can hear his lovely voice coming through his muscles and skin, through his shirt and jacket as she gazes with one inflamed eye at her mother.

Seeing

Pearl and her father had planned a walk through the beech woods, along the steep old lane and onto the mountain. Pearl wakes up thinking about the wood with its moving pools of bright, soft grass, its tawny sunlight and the small stands of hazel weighed down with new, furry-skinned, crushable nut clumps. She puts her walking clothes on and takes the stairs two at a time. In the kitchen her parents stand holding coffee cups. She looks from one to the other and sees that she won't be going out with her father today. I need her at home, that's all, her mother says as she leaves the room. Her father sips his coffee. Really, it's okay, Daddy, Pearl tells him, I understand. My good girl, he says. Then he puts his coat on and goes out alone. All through the long morning Pearl's throat burns, and it's as if wasps are buzzing around her. After lunch, Pearl has to keep her mother company while she knits. Perched on the settee, she listens to the tap-tap of the needles and looks down at her walking shoes. Then she starts to examine the huge, open lilies on the coffee table. Eventually her mother looks at them too, dropping her busy hands into her lap. What? she says, as Pearl leans forwards, transfixed by the flowers. What can you see? Pearl points silently, and turns her head slowly to look at her mother. Can't you see them? she asks. Can't you see them, Mother? Pearl's mother falls to her knees and puts her hands to her trembling lips. Itty-bitty snakes, Mother, Pearl says. Green snakelets, all weaving out of the mouths of the lilies. Can't you see them? And she points again. No, her mother whispers, hardly daring to look. Where, Pearl? Where?

Focus

Honey and Pearl share a table in Art class. This is serious, the teacher shouts from the front. This is your final exam. Focus, please. Pearl doesn't hear. She is working out how she can draw what she wants to draw without giving anything away. It's a game to her, and almost second nature. Big floppy knickers, says Honey, staring at her own huge sheet of paper. Unlike you, most inscrutable one, I don't have any secrets. I know, says Pearl, looking at Honey, but not looking. Poor you. Just make something up. You know: focus. Who the heck cares, anyway? Honey doesn't answer, though she knows Pearl cares very much about something. She might as well save her breath; Pearl never listens to anyone, ever. Quiet! the teacher shouts. You have three hours. Pearl holds her pencil loosely. She feels a warm current rushing from her heart, up through her throat and then, with a final spurt, flaring out from her two eyes. Her hair sparks with electricity. The three hours whiz by in a holy silence while Pearl creates her drawing. Here is the ink-black hair, here the strong, pliant neck. A naked back, perfect legs. Inhuman eyes; blank and brown. The page is hardly big enough for the unspeakable things she draws, as she smells a perfume sharply green. Then a humming sound fills her ears and she comes back to herself. Pearl! her teacher is calling, and shaking her shoulders. Whatever's the matter? Pearl asks, confused. I've finished, that's all, she says, and smiles as she puts down her pencil. There is silence in the classroom as everyone crowds near the table and examines Pearl's completely blank sheet.

All right

Now Pearl is older, it's hard to go on waiting for her plans to work out. There are times when she would like to shake her head and be free; if her silvery hair were a mane and she had hooves like a pony, she believes she could escape. Poor Pearl, she thinks, listening to the beat of her galloping hooves. All these weeks and months, all these buzzing little schemes to outrun. Time streaks ahead and blocks her path. But today is not one of those days. Today is like a glowing box that Pearl balances on the top shelf of her heart. At any moment the box might open, like a magical eyelid, and out would fly the wonderful things Pearl knows will happen if she tries hard enough. So she quivers, holding Will's hand as they walk along the abandoned canal path. It's late afternoon and over the mountains the sun moves in and out of a bank of churning cloud. Each time a finger of light breaks through, it touches the flanks of the mountain tenderly, illuminating secret folds and humps, and Pearl and Will point, shouting, there! there! to each other. They decide to walk up through a wheat field to the top. Pearl feels her way, hardly disturbing the shaggy stalks, unaware of Will's small voice calling, and soon she is alone, suspended in the shimmering field's hot, yeasty breath. Standing in the waist-high golden wheat, Pearl is aware of the smallest movement above her heart. Like a column of smoke, her hair lifts and lowers, her grey eyes take in the unquiet sky and the mountains blooming with sunbeams, and she knows that, eventually, everything will be all right.

Shed

Pearl's mother has been in bed for days. At least, she would be, if she didn't keep escaping. Pearl and her brother camp out in the garden shed. Pearl makes quick trips into the kitchen and steals food. Nobody notices. If Pearl peers in through the lounge window, she sees her father surrounded by strange people all talking at the same time. Poor Daddy, she says to her brother, as they share a tin of cold rice pudding. What will he do? Her brother doesn't know. They've got blankets and books in the shed. The smell of creosote and wood shavings makes it homely. Several times search parties are sent out to find their mother. She likes to throw her wedding ring in the river, or walk barefoot through the stores in town, searching for clocks. Often the children watch as she lurches like a broken kite around the garden, her nightdress half off, ripping flowers and slinging their torn heads over her shoulders. Pearl pulls her brother under the work-table when their mother is in the garden, and sings to him until she's recaptured. One evening they're washing in a plastic bowl Pearl's found, when they notice all the lights are on in the house. They hear shouting, and watch from the shed window as the back door is flung open and their mother twirls out into the dark, something long and thin glinting in her hand. She makes straight for the shed. Get down! Pearl whispers to her brother. Outside the slatted wooden walls Pearl can hear her mother's breathing and the sound of something metallic being dragged across the door. My Pearl! her mother calls. Are you in there? Come out! Pearl shields her brother, waiting for her father to come and save them.

The answer

Pearl has decided to stay at home instead of going to Granny's. She cleans the empty house. It's four o'clock now, so she bathes and washes her hair. Wrapped in a towel, she walks into her parents' bedroom and sits at the dressing table. It's years since she looked at all her mother's messy things. Pearl picks up a brush and examines it. Then she squirts herself with perfume. When she inhales she feels, for a second, as if her mother is standing behind her. It's always evening in this room, and the bed seems to float like a ghost ship in the gloom. Pearl walks to her father's side of the bed and pulls back the covers. She lifts the pillow, and without disturbing the neat folds, bends until her face is pressed into his pyjamas. Then she puts things back. In her mother's wardrobe the dresses wait, but after looking she leaves. Soon she's dressed and downstairs. It feels normal in the kitchen and Pearl stops thinking about the room above. When she hears her father's key in the door she calls, Are you hungry, Daddy? Sit down, and I'll take your shoes off. Her father rubs his forehead. The shadows under his eyes make her heart feel like an old, screwed-up paper bag. She sits on the floor and unties his laces while he strokes her damp hair. Then she jumps to her feet and takes two jacket potatoes out of the oven. She prepares one for him. Butter, Daddy? she asks quietly. And cheese too? You like cheese. Then she does her own. But he isn't eating, so she puts down her cutlery. Are you very tired of things as they are, Daddy? she asks him, and her heart expands like a scarlet paper flower when he looks at her and nods.

Blush

Pearl walks along the chemist shop aisles, humming the two-note song designed to drown out her mother's voice. Pearl can see the woman behind the pharmacy counter listening as her mother goes on and on, and the queue forming, and all she can do is drift around, pretending to be a normal customer, and wait. She stops in front of the make-up stand. These little vials and bottles and tubes. Pearl wonders about them. She picks up a tiny container of green, sparkly powder. Why would you put this on your eyelids? she thinks. Sniffing and squeezing, daubing improbable shades on the backs of her hands, she hums all the time. When she's squirted and smeared all that's available, she sees the pharmacy lady holding her mother's elbow and guiding her out of the shop, so she follows. Keeping her mother in sight, she puts a hand in the pocket of her jacket and feels the small pot she's taken. Her mother stops and waits for her. Pearl! she shouts, stamping her foot. Hands out! Shoulders back! Pearl looks beyond her mother, at the neat hedges either side of the road. For the rest of the way home her mother talks and Pearl hums loudly. She spends the remainder of the day in her bedroom. When it's nearly time to eat, she gets the pot out of her jacket pocket and unscrews the lid. She rubs her finger in the pink cream and applies it to her cheeks. Suddenly, her reflected eyes are more vivid, her lips defined and her skin looks creamy and plush. At the table she sees her mother's narrow-eyed look. Hello, Daddy, she says, and her smile broadens when he finally notices her and says, Pearl, go and wash that off. There's no need to gild a lily.

Broken

In the cinema, Pearl and Will snog. This film is stupid, Will says. We're a million times more interesting than that boring pair, don't you think? Pearl opens Will's trousers and clasps his penis in her hand. It seems to have a life all its own as it firms itself, pushing her fist open a little. She has her other arm draping his shoulders, and she looks at him as he rests his head against her neck. His closed lashes lie quietly, and the flickering lights from the screen gather in his sockets and run in and out of his half-open mouth. Pearl bends to kiss his face and waits for him to gasp and judder. Then she gives him a tissue. Sweet, sweet Will, she thinks, when he plants a kiss on her cold cheek. They struggle into their coats. Outside it's dark and still raining. As they walk to the bus stop the sky seems to lower itself over them, the clouds shouldering each other for space. Pearl holds Will's hand and looks at the undersides of the clouds. They're damaged-looking; pulpy, and the rain falling from them is dark, like juice. Everything appears stained and broken. The buildings seem abandoned. To Pearl, even the shop fronts look blank and boarded up. Will is telling her about a plan he has for the two of them, how it'll be fun. A car goes by, but Pearl can't see any driver inside. Stop, she says, as the rain goes on falling in the wet street. Now seems as good a time as any, she thinks, and in a few words tells Will they're finished. Is there someone else you love more than me? he asks, crying. Pearl looks tenderly at him. Yes, there is, she says, and wipes his tears with her hands.

New start

Pearl has been out of action for days. That's how she feels; like some seized-up, broken-down machine, good only to be thrown in the skip. When she thinks about Will, and the wet street, the lowering, swollen sky and how she ran away from his tearful question, something repeatedly clangs in her head like a swinging door deep inside a spooky house. She stays in her room, refusing to go to school. On the third day her mother comes in, leaning over to shout stuff about pulling herself together, and Pearl hits her with a book, telling her, flatly, to go to hell. Her mother's mouth opens and closes a few times – it's quite funny really, Pearl thinks – then she slaps Pearl so hard across the side of her head that she is almost knocked off the bed. Carefully right-ing herself, a comma of blood slipping from the corner of her closed mouth, she stares at her mother. Now look what you've done, she says, deliberately dribbling blood onto her chin. What do you imagine Daddy will say about this? The slap has been useful, Pearl realises. It's wedged that bonkers swinging door shut, and now she can start to think. The blow has woken her up, warmed her blood, set it flowing again. Her mother is still standing beside the bed, so Pearl tells her to drop dead. But Pearl, her mother says, don't speak to me that way. I won't allow it. She's gulping for air, and her hands are tightly twisted together. Say you're sorry, dear, she asks in a small voice. The imprint of the book has made a comic, tick-shape on her forehead. Come now, I know you don't mean it, she says, as Pearl begins to laugh bloodily.

Thinking

Pearl has been sent away. Alone, she trails about her granny's garden. Everything is dead. Even the beautiful dahlia heads look like soggy bunches of decaying hair now. There's a droning in her ears; she's scared of herself, and what will happen. It's as if her toes are on the very last, crumbling edge of something and she must make an impossible leap, or fall and disappear. Her granny is calling; it's time to eat. The kitchen table's set and the fire crackles and shifts. Pearl looks at the foamy, primrose-yellow omelette on her plate. I can't, she says. So her grandmother makes her a mug of hot chocolate. It's so delicious she drinks it all. Then they sit on the settee, and Pearl rests her head in her granny's soft lap. She thinks about Will, his dissolving smile in the rainy street and her mother always crying, or shouting, or talking to herself, until she begins to writhe secretly inside. And then she moves her thoughts away. Instead she closes her eyes and remembers her father, and their long ago, snowy walk. She pictures the lighted windows and the globes of teeming snowflakes like dandelion clocks surrounding the street lamps. Over and over she recalls the sound of her father's laugh when the woman asked, and is this your wife? Soon she feels herself uncoil. What are you thinking about, Pearl? her granny asks, seeing her smile. She rests her cool hand on Pearl's forehead. But no, she adds after a few moments, looking at Pearl's gleaming eyelids and closed, pink mouth. I think it's best you keep those thoughts to yourself – whatever they are.

Code

Fee is in love. She goes on and on about it, flapping her hands to emphasise certain important facts. Pearl half listens, looking at Fee's little face, how happy her toothy mouth seems, her freckled nose glistening. The boy is older than Fee. Do you think that matters? she asks Pearl. I mean, he probably thinks I'm still a child. Is that weird? Is what weird? Pearl says. Her mind is on other things. Age, my love, says Fee. Do age gaps matter when you're mad about someone? No, Pearl says. She is lying on a blanket in Fee's garden, her hair fanned out, the skirt of her dress crumpled at the tops of her legs. Age is nothing if you really, really love a person, she says drowsily. Fee gets up and goes into the house. Yes, but how do you know that? she asks when she gets back, handing over an ice-lolly casually; Pearl doesn't like to accept food from people. Fee can see she is concentrating on something, so she watches for a moment as Pearl pushes the tip of the yellow lolly in and out of her mouth; then she lightly touches Pearl's hand and says, you're right, of course. You know most things. Then she lies down on the blanket, happy Pearl is licking her lolly, and snuggles up. The truth is, Pearl states, shifting her arm to embrace Fee, absolutely nothing matters when you love someone. What? Fee asks, making small slurping noises, nothing? You can't help it, Pearl whispers. You can't be blamed, if you love someone. Five years, ten years, blah, blah, blah. Who cares? Not twenty though, Fee says decisively, that's beyond. Especially twenty, Pearl tells her. Especially.

Wrong

Pearl is still thinking about Will. About how sweet he always was. The way he made her feel wrapped up in the most comforting blanket ever. Since she finished with him, she's been chilly; trembling and starting at any little thing. As if a layer of skin has been pulled off. Now I don't feel so clever, she thinks, gazing from her window, or so brave. But that's stupid, she realises. I've always been brave and clever. Nothing changes me. Still, she feels empty and weightless, and she doesn't like it. Fee comes round and they sit on the floor, up against the chilly radiator. What's the matter, my love? Fee asks, holding Pearl's hand. Nothing, Pearl says, shaking herself free. It's not too late to say you were wrong, Fee says, twizzling her thin red hair around her fingers. Why don't you just go and tell him you made a mistake? Pearl is suddenly restless. She's tired of being squashed into her room, and of Fee's body resting against her. Fee with her stupid freckles and teeth. I don't remember asking your advice, Pearl states. Fee is startled. I only mean you could have been wrong, Fee says again. Pearl stands up and looks down at her. She hates the way Fee always leans her head to one side and tries to cover her teeth with her top lip when she's thinking. You should keep your mouth shut, she says in a louder voice. If I have been wrong, it was about you. Fee puts her hands to her cheeks and stares up at Pearl. I'm sorry, Fee says. Please don't be angry. Pearl opens her bedroom door and says softly, Fee, you can go now.

Burning

No matter what she does, it's impossible for Pearl to shake off the feeling that there's a raw, weeping patch growing on her heart, and someone is pressing on it. It's not as if I care about stuff, she thinks, but tonight, the burning starts the moment she lies down, and chews away until she jerks herself out of bed and runs to the open window. Below her the tight-shut buds of the red climbing rose look black, and the flouncy squares of night-scented stock near the house wilt under their own petalled breath. Moonlight has spread a clean cover over everything. Further away Pearl can see the woods, cool and indifferent, darker than the dark and sparkling sky, and she thinks it might be possible to sleep there. Wearing her trainers and a jumper, she descends the stairs, closes the front door and drifts along the garden path. The gate creaks, so, resting her hand on its top bar, she leaps over. The night is thick with the smell of plants and sleeping earth. Pearl wades through a knee-high mist that's hovering inches above the field. A breeze lifts her hair and licks her eyelids. Soon she's amongst the trees, and their silvery trunks sway to make space for her. She goes further in, searching for somewhere to rest. When she's walked for a long time, and the trees are unfamiliar, she stops. There, in the crook of an oak's roots, is a spot where she could lie down. But as Pearl settles herself and closes her eyes, she sees Fee's hands flying to her mouth, and hears, threading through the calm, unknowable woods, Fee's shaky voice calling out that she's sorry, and the burning begins again.

Bikini

Pearl and Honey are shopping in town. What I really want, Honey says, is a freakishly stunning cossie. So they go to the swimwear section of a huge store. Pearl is silently amazed at the hundreds of different swimming costumes. Hers is an ancient Speedo, with a worn, transparent patch that shows the ghostly cheeks of her bottom. Until now she'd thought it looked great on her. Try some on, Honey says, her arms full of slithery scraps of fabric. It'll be a hoot. But Pearl doesn't answer. Come in with me anyway, Honey calls. So she sits in the changing room and passes items, watching as Honey poses in all sorts of costumes, slapping her bare bottom each time Honey bends over. Ow, Honey says, on cue, after each soft slap. Well? What do you think? she asks at last, posing in a splashy-patterned floral number. Pearl looks Honey up and down and turns her round for inspection. Yes, she nods finally, her hands still on Honey's shoulders. I would even say this one's freakishly stunning. Okay, Honey says, that's decided. Don't you want something to wear this summer? she asks, putting her knickers back on. You've got a gorgeous body. We could go to the lido together. She jiggles her purse. I've got loads of moolah, if you want some. But Pearl just shakes her head, pushing her hands into the pockets of her jeans. On the way home on the bus, Pearl watches the people rushing past and thinks about the black bikini she saw, with its eyelets and laces between the breasts and on the front of the panties. And how much she wants it.

Thigh

Pearl is having one of those nights when she repeatedly dreams the same thing; there is the same party going on, with the same music, and she's pushing through the dancers, looking for someone. Then there is a loud series of knocks, and she knows that something unstoppable and terrifying is about to begin. Her father is suddenly by her side, dragging her by the hand while the music howls and the dancers laugh and point. Pearl screams, No! Daddy, no! But her father flings open the door. There, doffing his hat, is a man with a huge head and a tiny body. He doesn't have a real mouth, just a painted smile on his egg-shaped face. I've come for her, he says, pointing elaborately at Pearl with a white-gloved finger. Can't you see what's happening? Pearl screams, struggling to hold onto her father, but he laughs, shoving her out into the dark. As the door slams Pearl wakes up with wet cheeks. Each time she falls asleep the dream starts again. Finally, she gets up and silently darts across the landing into her parents' room. She clambers onto their bed and eases herself in between them. Pearl's mother mumbles for her to get out, but her father shifts to make room. Let her stay, he says. Let her stay. Pearl is safely wedged between her parents, with only her sharp nose out in the cold. As her feet grow warm she becomes aware of her mother's naked thigh, glassily smooth and cool, pressing against her. Pearl shrinks from her mother's flesh, towards her father. She takes a fold of his pyjamas between her thumb and finger and rubs the silky fabric until she falls asleep.

Forgiven

Pearl squats on the back door step and contemplates how boring the whole Fee thing is. Each time she's come round, Pearl has refused to see her. In school she behaves as if Fee is a stranger. Every time Fee tries to slip in beside her in class, Pearl slings her bag on the chair. Fee's little sagging shoulders and pink eyes leave Pearl unmoved. When Fee tries to say how sorry she feels about what she said, Pearl sings her two-note song. Digging a thumbnail into the soft wood at the bottom of the doorframe, Pearl wonders if friends are worth the trouble. She gazes down the garden to the hedge they used to play under. Pearl thinks about those times. Everything was simple then, she tells herself, even though she knows it's not true. Suddenly she gets up and walks across the lawn. The gap they crawled through is overgrown, but she squeezes in and rearranges the branches, hugging her knees in the tiny space, remembering how it felt to be in the hedge's heart. She pictures Fee, snivelling as she chewed mud cakes stuck with insects, her mouth smeared with gravel. She remembers Fee's thin wrist, and her silence when Pearl gave her a Chinese burn. Pearl closes her eyes, and sees her friend Fee smiling. She can almost hear her saying hello, my love. Something is stuck like a half-swallowed wodge of gum in Pearl's throat. She gulps hard and opens her eyes. There on the dry earth is a shrivelling bunch of fern tips and campion, with a scrap of paper from Fee that she hadn't noticed before. I suppose I will forgive her, Pearl decides, looking at the bouquet through stinging eyes. Even though she doesn't deserve it.

Where?

Pearl starts to disappear from school at lunchtime. Fee and Honey are watchful, but one minute she's, say, swinging her bag at someone, and the next, poof! she's gone. Or just as everyone's struggling into the canteen, bang! they realise she's not there. In afternoon class, Fee steals looks at Pearl, trying to work out where she's been. But Pearl's profile tells her nothing. Her straight nose is concentrating on the teacher and without looking at the page she doodles her favourite fern and fish shapes as usual. Once, she turned her strange, light eyes on Fee and pinched her hand with an understanding look. Fee and Honey are so puzzled they finally decide to split up and search everywhere. After a first sweep they meet on the field. I think you should be the one to ask her, Fee states, shuddering. She's been angry with me recently. I certainly will not, Honey says, giving her thick hair a shake. Pearl never answers questions. You know how she is. I don't understand what you mean, Fee says, carefully covering her jutting teeth with her top lip. Honey sighs and drops onto the daisies. Don't pretend Pearl's like other people, she says. It's just not true. She's, well, a bit weird sometimes. They sit facing each other and fall silent. Now I feel guilty, talking like this, Fee says, thinking about Pearl, her determined aloneness. And me, Honey answers, and gets up. See you, she calls as she runs off. Weeks go by and still Pearl is nowhere to be seen at lunchtime. Then, just as suddenly, she's back. A little thinner, Fee thinks, and maybe happier. As if something she's wished for has come true.

Picnic

Pearl is in Will's kitchen. After a long month she has agreed they can still be friends. Let's make a picnic, he says. We can go anywhere you want. Pearl sits on the table, swinging her bare legs. So, what's your favourite food? he asks. Pomegranates and black grapes, she says. Will is disappointed. Anything else? he asks, stroking her arm, smiling brightly. She considers. I like chicken, if you must know. And peaches. And cheese. Will looks carefully at her. Really? he says. I only ask because that's what I have here. Perfect then, Pearl answers, tapping him lightly on the nose. We'll take this wine, Will goes on, pulling a bottle out of the fridge. My mother'll never notice. He packs a rucksack. Follow me, Pearl says. She leads him across the field, through the ferns, down to the stream. They take their tops off and stand in the water with their arms by their sides. Pearl makes her new breasts, with their tiny nipples, nudge Will's chest. You are beautiful, Will whispers. Pearl stoops and splashes him, and her laughter seems to intensify the sunlight glinting through the trees. They hold hands and she takes him deeper into the woods. They come to a clearing covered with dry, rust-coloured beech leaves. A golden silence lies over every surface. Will spreads a blanket as Pearl takes off her shorts. Me too, he says and strips quickly. They spread out on their backs in the sunshine, swigging the chilly white wine and eating peaches. Wood pigeons call throatily to each other. Now and then a breeze strokes the trees above. This is nice, Pearl says. Time to turn over. We have to do both sides.

Introductions

Pearl's mother is pretending to make a cake. Some of these, she says, accurately flicking eggs still in their shells into a big bowl. Puffs of flour spurt as each egg breaks. And some of these, she laughs, emptying a bag of dried onion pieces on top. Especially nice, she explains to the empty room, because they're like scrunched-up insects. Pearl has been watching from the hallway. As her mother shoots a stream of tomato ketchup into the bowl, she walks into the kitchen. Watcha doin'? she asks, tapping her mother briskly on top of the head. Trying to kill us all? Her mother freezes, hands clasped around the plastic bottle. She looks cornered, but Pearl takes juice from the fridge and drinks it from the carton, ignoring her. Don't, her mother says, licking her lips: it's not nice. Who says? Pearl asks. Her mother is shuffling her feet, and craning to see something on a shelf above Pearl's head. *She* did, she announces, and points the bottle towards the cover of a cookery book. Just visible is the face of a smiling woman. Oh, really? Pearl asks. Is she your friend? Her mother folds into a chair and puts the bottle down. I suppose she gave you this brilliant recipe, Pearl says. Her mother is whispering behind her hands. I don't think she can hear you, Mother, she tells her loudly. Speak up! Her mother points again. This is a girl whose name is Pearl, her mother calls to the photograph. I don't know what she's doing in this house. Pearl does an elaborate flourish and indicates her mother to the book. And this is a madwoman no one wants, she says. How we all wish she'd disappear.

Saving

Pearl walks to town, down the long, swooping road bordered with weeds that in summer will have moving clumps of ladybirds hanging from their branches. Over the bridge she goes, past the nursery school, its play yard twitching with tiny figures, and down into the underpass. Her pocket is heavy with coins. Not for one minute was she tempted to buy even a stick of gum with her lunch money. For one hour every school day, while the sun gleamed above her, or rain fell, she rested in the secret place she'd found and thought of nothing. Each morning, there was her lunch money, on the table in the hall. And now she has enough. It's quiet and almost empty in the store. Assistants admire themselves in mirrors, but Pearl doesn't look at them as she travels up the escalator and walks into the swimwear section. Soon, she's on her way home again, the store bag pushed inside her jacket. There's the evening meal to get through. Her mother serves them food that looks as if it came from a joke shop. Pearl looks at the shiny, garish mounds of vegetables. Seriously? she says to her mother, holding up a charred chop. Can't I have bread and cheese? Something real? She swerves neatly when her mother leans across to slap her face. Nothing for you then, her mother shouts, covering the plates with thick gravy. Her brother rhythmically kicks the table leg as he eats, but Pearl does nothing. All she can think of is getting to her bedroom and closing the door. It's almost too perfect; there, on her bed, is the tiny black bikini with silver eyelets and laces. Just waiting to be put on.

Goodbye

In a scramble of knickers is a heap of assorted bones. Pearl closes her drawer and hums to keep her spirits up. Then later, she spots a finger bone poking out of the mouth of her trainer. She remembers, long ago, how it felt when she first saw the skeleton girl point at her from inside the school hall curtains. Now, tidying up, she smiles, thinking about how her skeleton girl was always around; splashing in the stream, hanging from a door hook, nodding yes, yes, from the undergrowth, tinkling and clattering, willing to play whenever she was needed. Settling into bed she finds, like a question mark, a collarbone under the pillow, so she goes downstairs. In the kitchen sink the cold tap drips into the blind eye of an empty pot as Pearl takes an apple and walks out into the moon-haunted garden. Now she's older, her skeleton girl rarely appears in one piece, and that's understandable. It's hard to imagine those years when they spent so much time together. Then suddenly, Pearl recalls a lovely hour when they sat smiling on a high ledge somewhere, listening to the hollow bang of sheep's jaws bouncing across the dark forestry. The fir tree by the back door exhales a melancholy breath as Pearl brushes past, linking then and now. On the garden path she can just make out a trail of white fragments. They are the skeleton girl's teeth, leading her, so she follows. At the end of the path is a cherry tree, knobbly with buds, each twig sheathed in moonlight. Through her tears, Pearl sees, at the end of one branch, her dear girl's bony little hand, waving goodbye for good.

Nothing

Some nights, Pearl hears sounds she doesn't like. When she was little, she'd stuff her bunny right up between her legs and squeeze him rhythmically until a shimmer flooded first her belly, then her chest and she couldn't hear the sounds she didn't like any more. When she was older, Pearl forced a pillow over her head and whispered to herself, it's okay, it's nothing, it's okay, it's nothing, until she fell asleep again. Tonight, Pearl is lying in bed, her eyes stretched to the dark. Something has woken her. In her head a familiar feeling begins to develop, and to stop it Pearl gets up to look outside. It's a summer night. She opens the window wide and climbs onto the inside sill. Even behind the curtain, leaning out to sniff the faint, steady breath of the quiet woods, Pearl can still hear. Enough, she says quietly, and jumps down. The lace curtains at the landing window throw ragged grey patterns onto her face as she stands outside the door to her parents' room. This is where the sounds come from. Pearl feels as if her heart will shatter. The sighs and grunts she hears are like the noises a huge lie would make. But this can't be right, she thinks, and opens the door so violently that it bangs a chair. She sees, without looking, the squirming bed, and her mother's naked leg thrown out from under the covers. Her father's strong back is facing her, skewed to one side. Daddy! Be quiet! she shouts. Then, somehow, she's back in her own room, and the sounds have stopped. It's okay, it's nothing, she tells herself, as she falls asleep, it's absolutely nothing. It's okay.

Wow

Finally the day comes when her mother and brother will both be out. At breakfast it's touch and go, so Pearl thinks about nothing. What will you two do this fine day? her mother asks. Her father reads the paper. Stuff, Pearl says, watching the sunlight wink on her knife. What sort of stuff? her mother asks, her head to one side like some huge bird. Dunno, Pearl answers, sipping juice. This is the crucial moment, so she acts bored. What about you? Her mother pokes a finger into the newspaper's centre crease so it collapses. She's trying to sound chirpy, but Pearl knows what's going on. Oh, her father says, folding the paper. Gardening, I think. And will you help, madam? her mother asks. Nope, Pearl answers. It's almost midday before the house is empty. Pearl stands in the bathroom listening to her father's spade clink against stones. Opening the window she watches as he wipes his forehead. Sit on the bench, Daddy, she calls. I'll bring you a drink. He wears shorts and his legs are surprising. She glimpses his navel when he lifts the spade onto his shoulder. Sounds good, he says and walks into the shade of the apple trees. Quickly Pearl changes and gets the drinks. She carries the tray into the dappled cover of the trees. Her father is lying on the bench, his boots and shirt beside him. Daddy! Do you like my bikini? she calls, and waits. Her father sits up and looks at Pearl's small, full breasts held neatly in the black cups, her perfect brown legs, her tender, flat stomach. Well? she says, swishing her hair, still holding the tray. Wow, her father mouths, his hands open on his knees.

Trip

Today, some of the old gang are going to the beach. Will has a car now and they intend to cram themselves in with all their stuff. Pearl doesn't speak on the long journey; this is the first time she can remember going to the coast. At last they park and walk through the dunes. The shifting bosoms of sand, the white birds like air-blown, musical blossoms, the sound of the invisible sea, all held inside the huge, upturned bowl of the sky, send Pearl into a kind of rapt absence. Then they're on the beach. Miles of cream-and-blue loveliness stretch out before Pearl, and her throat bubbles with a feeling she can scarcely hold. Honey gets into her new bikini quickly, but Pearl still wears her old costume. They decide to eat first, and quickly lay out a picnic, but Pearl isn't hungry. Instead she wants to walk on the rocks and explore the pools with their fringes of purplish grass. Everything seems to squirt, or shrink, or liquefy when she touches it, unlike anything she's ever seen or felt before. The smell of the wrack, the tough capsules of seaweed that burst with a wet plop, the plant ropes covered in orange warts and especially the transparent, darting pool life, Pearl looks at them all. Suddenly, she stands up and feels a flash behind her eyes; the vast, lemony sky and the heaving disk of the sea all blend into one inexpressible, sparkling new idea of the world. With closed eyes she searches for her dim and rustling woods, the bright stream, her swaying ferns, for her mother's red face in the steamy kitchen and for a moment, it's a struggle to remember.

Disappointment

Pearl carries inside her now the yelling gulls and wheat-coloured dunes pierced by tough bristles of marram grass. More than anything else, there are miles of wind-scooped beach stretching out, waiting for her to run over them any time she wants. When Will stops the car for something to eat, Pearl realises she is ravenous. The windows mist with a vinegary fug as everyone eats fish and chips and swigs Coke, and they all laugh at Pearl's concentration on her food. Her lips shine as she smiles, waggling a drooping chip. I love the beach, Honey says with her mouth full. It rocks. And they all laugh again. Soon it's quiet and only Pearl and Will stay awake. When she gets home eventually and climbs out of the car, Pearl feels loose-limbed, and her hair is so stiff it looks powdered. The idea of going into any of those tiny rooms is almost impossible, but she forces herself to step inside. It's quiet, yet Pearl can sense they are all waiting for her. In the lounge her brother crouches on the carpet. He looks mutely at her. Sitting either side of the empty fireplace are her parents. Her mother is tensed, ready to leap from her chair. Pearl looks at her father, but he is studying his locked hands. For a moment they all look like strangers. Is something wrong, Daddy? she asks. You could say that, madam, her mother answers in an oddly deep voice, waving the two pieces of the black bikini between fingers and thumbs as if they were filthy rags. What have you got to say about this disgusting thing? And don't speak to your father, she adds, a vibration in her voice. He is very disappointed in you.

Moving on

Pearl gathers up the bikini fragments strewn on the carpet and stuffs them in her pocket. Jacketless, she leaves the house, head down, oblivious to the evening, or to where she's going. Her shoes darken at the tips as she crosses a field and a wet wind blows her hair across her face, then changes direction, whipping it all out behind her like a signpost. She reruns in her head the huge, black-handled scissors, her mother chopping haphazardly at the bikini. I'm doing this for your own good! she'd shouted, pulling the delicate laces from their eyelets and snipping them into finger-length sections, unaware she was cutting her own dress at the same time. No one is interested in you, Pearl! she'd said. No one! As Pearl watched, she'd felt herself shrinking to the size of a gnat. She could clearly see her brother trying to grab the bikini, and hear her father shout as he struggled to get control of the scissors. She zoomed closer as they tussled. It looked as if her father would not be strong enough to wrest open her mother's fists. Pearl could feel herself buzzing, circling, invisible to all of them. Then she landed, back in her old self, and the room was empty, everything just the same, but for an overturned chair and the litter of black scraps on the floor. Now, on the side of the grey-toned mountain, Pearl stops walking and empties her pockets. In brilliant colour she sees her house: the apple trees in the garden, the tray with two glasses, the sunlight sparking along the blades of grass, her father on the bench, silently mouthing WOW, and realises that the bikini's not important any more.

Silver birches

Pearl wakes up to a commotion. It's like the shifting clamour of a huge, angry crowd. But how come? she thinks. I'm alone in my room. She checks outside. Through her window the dark street is familiarly empty. In the house beyond her bedroom door the furniture sleeps, rugs sprawl out on floors and she can just imagine the fridge's lonely night-time buzz. The noise must be inside her head. It's a startling thought. She lies down and tries to work it out. Even with her eyes tightly shut she can tell that the room is shifting to another colour. And that she is not alone. The clatter in her head is gone. In its place is a whispering sound, as if millions of tiny palms were softly clapping. She opens her eyes. Her room is full of saplings whose bright trunks are festooned with silky tatters. They all incline towards her. The nearest lean over her bed on three sides and dangle their stippled, minutely jointed branches onto the covers. The semi-dark is like the clearing in a tall forest; sharp with green smells and the serious perfume of dripping moss. The trees are swaying. It seems to Pearl that they are saying, ressstt, as they dangle their serrated, heart-shaped leaves across her forehead and cheeks. Everything is goooood. Pearl falls asleep again, lulled by the birches' woody music. When she wakes in the morning, she stretches. There on the covers is a withered, broken twig. Suddenly she remembers the night, and an unwelcome new thought bashes her smartly across the head. Maybe the trees were giving her a warning? But, Pearl wonders, whatever could it be?

The future

Mr Wilks, the form teacher, is explaining to Pearl about the importance of her exams. You're very bright, he says, wiping the board. Have you thought much about your future? Pearl's perched on a desk, her forthright eyes on him. She could laugh, she thinks, at such a question. Why are you smiling? Mr Wilks asks. Pearl sits quietly, her hair illuminating the drab room, and contemplates all the rooms just like this one, all the lessons she's sat through, all the workbooks and tests, all the ticks and crosses. I'm just thinking about school, she says. And is it funny? her teacher asks. In a way, Pearl says, slipping off the desk neatly. On the way home Pearl walks through the park, swinging her bag. She balances on the kerb and feels the huge chestnut trees looming over her. The evening light is making every surface look soft and frayed, as if instead of wood, say, or metal, it were covered in worn-out fabric. School is hilarious, she thinks, but it's also sad. Everybody is working so hard, and for what? She feels sorry for the teachers. Soon, school will be over for ever. In the end, all the children there will scatter. It's as if her real life can't begin until a few things are in place, and leaving school is one of them. When she gets home, her father is already in. She tells him about Mr Wilks and he looks serious. Do you care about exams, Daddy? she asks. Honestly, why do I need qualifications for what I'm going to do? Her father takes hold of her hands. And what might that be, my good girl? he asks, smiling. Pearl is intensely surprised. But Daddy, she says, don't you know yet?

Tablets

Pearl hovers outside her mother's room, scooting downstairs as the door opens. In the hall her father is shaking the doctor's hand. Those should do the trick, the doctor says, as he leaves. She must take them regularly. Pearl comes out from behind the kitchen door when her father calls. He wants her to go to the pharmacy. The sooner she starts on this medication, he says, the better. Be quick, my good girl. Pearl dawdles to the shops. It's a windy day and there seem to be hundreds of birds flying around. Pearl thinks of a time when she'd have imagined a golden eagle swooping to snatch the prescription out of her fingers and take it to line a magnificent nest. But that doesn't work any more. She queues in the chemist. On the way home she stops in the park to investigate the medicine. Twirling on a deserted roundabout, she opens the boxes: just two-tone pellets encased in plastic. It's hard to believe they have the power to pull her mother back. And Pearl knows her mother will not want to take them. There is a commotion in the bedroom as Pearl's father tries to get her mother to swallow the pills. He looks exhausted when he comes downstairs. Pearl hands him a cup of tea and a biscuit. Don't you worry about it, Daddy, she tells him. I'll give them to her if you like. I'd like to help. A week goes by. Pearl has been spending time, twice a day, with her mother. Pearl sits on the bed and opens her hand to reveal the tablets. With a hand firmly over her mouth her mother looks at them, then watches as Pearl puts the tablets back in her pocket, and leaves, gently closing the door.

The walk

Pearl had to stretch out on the floor of her room to do up the zip of her new jeans. She'd posed in front of the mirror and nodded at the slim stalks of her legs. If only I didn't have to wear a top, she thought, or this hospital-looking bra. My breasts are so nice. But who in this neighbourhood walks out with their boobs on show? Still, the bonus is that God, or Someone, had answered her prayers and given her small, pinky-tipped nipples, instead of those elongated brown jobs her mother's saddled with. Now it's late in the afternoon and she waits outside the place her father works. Finally, she sees him. But instead of his usual smooth, elegant walk, he's limping. For a moment, everything freezes. She has to think hard about her father with a limp. No, she thinks, it's okay. The limp makes him look even better, maybe. And it probably won't be for ever. Immediately, the bunchy arms of the trees in the gardens, and the still cars in the road, all start moving again. Pearl hides until her father passes, then falls in far enough behind to be unnoticed. As they walk, Pearl is in a reverie. She only sees her father and the unfamiliar way he moves. Soon she starts to mimic the strange shape his leg makes. On they go, her father first, limping. Then, far behind, Pearl in her new, tight jeans, with avid eyes, limping too, until they are nearly home. Suddenly, Pearl straightens and sprints, taking another route, and throws herself on the settee moments before her father gets in. Good evening, Daddy, she says. Everything all right with you? I had a feeling something might be wrong.

Sounds

Pearl's father clears his throat. It's as if what he wants to say is paralysing his tonsils. Poor Daddy, Pearl thinks, trying her best to understand him. He gets up and walks to the window, running his fingers through his floppy black hair. Finally it becomes clear. He wants Pearl to listen to something her mother has to say. Do you understand how things have gone too far? he asks Pearl, striding back to hold her fists in his strong hands. Please talk to your mother. So Pearl kisses his cheek. Is that all? she thinks, climbing the stairs to her parents' room. Inside, she walks straight to the window and throws it open wide. Fresh, gusty air blows in. Well? she says, sitting at the bottom of the bed. Her mother arranges herself and pulls the covers up to her chin, gesturing for Pearl to come nearer. Then she proceeds to talk. Pearl watches her mother's lips make shapes, and sees her moving her hands, but nothing makes sense. All she can hear are a series of clicks and whines, and the sound of breath rushing in and out. Finally, she's had enough and stands up. Her mother's eyes are glittering and she's nodding her head. Pearl locks herself in the bathroom and sits on the loo until she hears her father call. In the kitchen he's made a pot of tea. There are biscuits laid out. That was great, Pearl says, sitting down and pouring herself a cup. Really, really great. She sips and watches her father, her heart so clogged with sadness she begins to feel nauseous. He seems to be studying her. Pearl picks up the plate. Won't you have a biscuit, Daddy? she says, waving them in front of him. Go on, you deserve one.

Results

Pearl had stayed up, night after night, revising. The less she'd slept, the more she felt able to absorb all the stupid stuff she needed to remember. She'd lived on bananas and water. Finally, exam fortnight came. In school, everyone was either silent and grey, or yelling and laughing like fools. Pearl didn't speak to anyone. In her house, no one registered it was the end of term. Every time Pearl stepped outside, she plunged into another world where timetables and pens, schedules and forms were important. On the first day, she'd seen Fee hunched on her seat in the huge hall, shoulders heaving. Pearl could hear her gasps and nose-blowing from where she sat waiting for the exam to begin. Then, suddenly, it was all over. In the weeks while everyone waited for their results, Pearl forgot about the whole thing. Now, on a sunny morning, Fee calls. Are you coming? she says. Where are you going? Pearl asks. To get our results! Fee tells her. Aren't you nervous? You go on, Pearl says. She packs a rucksack and makes her way to a place in the woods where there is a perfect oval of bright, tender grass. She threads her way through the cool, whispering trees and listens to the birds singing about mysterious things she will never know. She spreads her blanket and lies down, watching the restless leaves break and regroup. When dusk fills the undergrowth, she retraces her steps. In the post a few days later, her results arrive. Are you pleased, Daddy? she asks. Her father is smiling widely. Yes, he says. You are a clever girl, and hugs her. That's all right then, Pearl says, hugging him back.

Bang

Pearl won't be allowed to have the radio on any more. Especially not Radio One. Her mother's brain can't take it, apparently. Pearl and her brother have been summoned to the lounge. There are far too many drums banging, and long words, their mother explains. I feel my head will explode. Of course, my love, their father murmurs, stroking her hands. No one is going to make you listen to the radio. He looks across at Pearl, and she forces herself to smile back. You two can go now, their mother tells them, falling back on the settee. Upstairs, Pearl screams into her pillow and pulls out a few strands of her silvery hair. She loves the radio; all those serene voices telling her about wars and famine, droughts and earthquakes. Everything goes on, just the same, in the beautiful world, and Pearl likes to hear people telling her about it. Mostly she loves Radio One. The ridiculous chat, Pearl finds it soothing, and the heavy-metal groups. The rhythms that send her mother into fits make Pearl happy. She wipes her eyes when she hears her father's knock at the door, and then tells him to come in. He's brought her the radio. But I'm not supposed to listen any more, Daddy, she says, her heart giving a little bright pulse as he stands holding out the radio to her. I thought you could have it on quietly in the shed, he says, handing her a pack of batteries. Oh, Pearl says. Okay. Then, because he looks so crestfallen, she gives him a hug. Thank you, Daddy, she says. When he's gone she chucks the radio in a corner and drops to the floor, banging her head on the wooden boards until she blanks out.

Couple

Pearl feels as if her body has been prone on the bedroom floor while her mind's travelled to another planet. Anyway, she's back now, and it's no surprise how the usual things are still going on. Her brother's in his room, drawing space-ships. Nice, she says, picking up a few sheets from the pile by the side of his bed. These are good, she adds. He looks pleased, and starts to explain about thrusters and jets, why he's added this particular vent here, not there. Whoa, Pearl says. You don't have to tell me, I know why you draw this stuff. In the lounge, her mother is lying on the settee, fingering her favourite towel. Pearl watches for a moment. She won't have a blanket, her father says, standing in front of the empty fireplace. It just has to be that towel. Never mind, Daddy, Pearl tells him. As long as she's quiet. She backs out of the lounge; it feels too crowded. I'm sure you're right, she hears her father call as she slams the front door. In the street Pearl has to wait until everything stops wobbling and heaving. She wonders why she feels so odd. It's as if all the red-brick houses are locked, their windows barred. The grass on the field looks scorched. Pearl steadies herself. Coming towards her up the street are two people with their arms wrapped around each other. She looks again. The girl has familiar thick, swishy hair. Honey? Pearl says as they slow down in front of her. Now I understand, she thinks. Here are Will and Honey, looking guilty, clutching each other. So you two are a couple now, she says, trying to take it in. Then she's back in her own room, and she doesn't know how she got there.

Hungry

Lying on her bed, Pearl realises that more and more often she feels like the only survivor of a shipwreck. Here she is, gripping a plank on an unfriendly ocean. Her swollen tongue hangs out of her mouth like a sand-filled sock. Her waterlogged feet are flapping, and her eyelashes are crusted with salt. The sun bakes her skin and frazzles her hair. And I can never go back, she thinks. Already it's too complicated, everything feels likes a knotted, snarled-up ball of wool. She thinks about Will, her friends and her mother, and realises that, if she'd really been shipwrecked, then all the people who were with her on board would have been saved. They're gone. Only Pearl, with her little secret and her roaring, stubborn, hungry heart would still be missing. I am the original drifting, hollow girl, she thinks, spread out in the ocean's arms. Pearl looks at herself on her plank, and soon she hears the seagulls laughing. The sea spray is stroking her skin and over the edge of the plank, below the surface of the colourless water, there are smiling fish flicking about. Her head feels light as a handful of seeds and her eyes are dazzled. All around, the scintillating sea is murmuring to her, and Pearl catches its meaning now and then. She sits up and stretches her arms to the horizon. Here there is no one to get in her way. This is okay, she thinks. In fact, this is more beautiful than anywhere else. Even the emptiness that sits like a yawning mouth in her chest makes everything sharper, more real. I am lucky, she thinks, settling down to sleep. It won't be much longer and this hunger will be gone.

Fight

Pearl waits for Honey outside the school gates. What do you want? Honey asks. She'd turned a little pale when she saw Pearl, but soon recovered herself. I want you, Pearl says. They walk in silence, while fat raindrops slap the pavement. Honey swings her bag, walking quickly. Without appearing to rush, Pearl keeps abreast. When they get to the park gates, Honey stops. So, she says. What is this about? Pearl puts her bag down. I think you know, she answers. I don't, Honey says, now flushing darkly. If it's because I'm going out with Will, then who cares? You've finished with him. That's not the point, Pearl says, feeling as if a strobe of light has her locked in its beam. There's a hissing sound all around her. She can see Honey's lips moving, but she doesn't hear any words. From her stomach a wave of energy is rising. When it reaches her head she strikes Honey so hard across her cheek that she falls to the ground. Pearl stands poised. Honey shakily gets to her feet. When she's upright, Pearl smacks her again, and this time, as her hand comes into contact with Honey's face, there's a cracking noise. Honey falls like a slim, chopped tree, and lies without moving on the wet tarmac. A baby's bottle half filled with curdled milk rolls towards her head and Pearl kicks it away. Then she kneels and pulls a few leaves from Honey's tumbled, gleaming hair. Pearl's face is expressionless. Honey stirs and manages to sit up, blood oozing from her nose. Pearl stands over her. You're mad, Honey cries furiously. Don't I know it, Pearl answers, and walks away.

Right as rain

Things have been veering madly in Pearl's house. Her father is not working; he has to be around now. Pearl can see that all the practical things that should be done are tossed aside these days. She and her brother stumble over unwashed bed linen. Dirty plates pile up. I hate this marge stuff, her brother announces, inspecting the toast Pearl brings him. No butter for us at the mo, she says. Pearl's mother is out of sight, in her bedroom. Pearl waits and watches. She and her brother spend all their time hiding. You can call me The Blob again if you like, her brother says, while they sit in the shed eating apples. Pearl looks at him. His legs are longer than hers now, and one of his trainers has a gaping seam. I will if you want me to, she answers. Now out, she adds. Find your friends. Surrounded by tools and shavings, she is almost asleep when her father comes out to the shed. How are things, kiddies? he asks quietly. He hunkers down and realises Pearl is alone. I'm fine, Daddy, she tells him, watching as he pushes a hand through his hair, as if ridding it of something. Your mother'll soon be as right as rain, he tells her. Now she's got you to help her with the tablets. Pearl looks at him steadily. We'll be a proper family again, he tells her. He slowly straightens, and Pearl gives him her hand so he can help her. As soon as she's upright she hugs him fiercely. He feels slighter than usual, and almost floppy. She pulls back. Her father's eye sockets are smudged, his hair disarranged. So she hugs him harder, and thinks about the piles of tablets in their plastic sheaths she's already thrown away.

Help

There's a knock at the front door and The Blob calls for Pearl to come down. She's been shut in her cupboard trying to read by the light of her dying torch. She blinks as she gets to the door; her eyes feel as if the pupils are wide open, and she can't make out for a moment who's standing there. It's me, Will says. I need to talk to you. Pearl narrows her eyes, trying to bring him into focus. He waits for her to speak. Eventually she says, well? Out with it. Will tells her he's come about her attack on Honey. Pearl looks blank. What made you do it? Will asks. It was cruel. Pearl holds up her hand, half smiling. What are you talking about? she asks. Will folds his arms, his face serious. This is not funny, Pearl, he says. The least you can do is apologise to Honey. Pearl is puzzled. Will looks like a person she might have seen somewhere, maybe in a magazine, someone vaguely familiar. She almost says, do I know you? but realises it would sound too weird. Behind Will, at the gate, stands a person. Pearl, Will says. Look at her. Look at who? Pearl asks. At Honey, Will says loudly, and he points to the figure at the gate. Pearl can see a girl with two black eyes and a cut face. I don't see what this has to do with me, she tells Will, starting to close the door. Will jams his foot in the gap, and attempts to hold Pearl's hand. Is there someone you can talk to? he asks. I think you need help. Pearl swings the door open so that he staggers towards her. Go, she says, pushing him away. I have never needed any help from anyone. Then she watches Will walk back to Honey before quietly closing the door.

Comfort

Pearl begins to believe there is nowhere she can safely go. The house is cold, its surfaces unreflecting, the cushions lumpy. The mirrors give back only misty versions of people. Her room is like a cell. She can feel damp air playing on her face when she lies in bed. When she wakes her hair is kinky. The contents of her cupboard and wardrobe are strewn like so much rubbish all over the floor. She detects a funny smell, and spends hours searching for its cause. Finally she gets a big screwdriver from the shed and prises off the skirting boards. Then a steady, chill breeze blows in at ankle height, and the smell of slugs and earwigs intensifies. She finds it almost impossible to walk through the woods now. Her legs look the same, but she feels so weak she can barely force them to carry her. In amongst the trees she stumbles, her stupid, dragging feet easily caught in brambles and clumps of grass. She is distressed to realise she might even fall, here in the woods, of all places. So she decides to pack her rucksack and walk around the streets all day. Further and further she walks, until she is in unknown neighbourhoods. One day she finds herself outside Nita's house, and knocks on the door. Ken answers. Can I come in? she asks. The familiar smell she likes creeps over Pearl, lessening the stiffness in her shoulders. Nita is out, Ken says. He sits opposite her and rubs his knees. I'll wait, she answers, giving him a level look. You won't be needing your stick, Ken, will you? she says, sighing deeply as she lays herself out on the settee. Before he can answer, she's fallen asleep.

Blame

Pearl is curled up in her cupboard again. Even with a pillow over her head she can hear The Blob sobbing. Apart from that, there is silence upstairs. She can sense her father pacing the lounge below; moving to the window, then away again. La-la, la-la, she sings under her breath. Easing herself out of the cupboard, she slips across the landing and walks into her mother's room. Who is it? her mother asks, trying to sit up. Pearl perches next to her. Not long now, Pearl says, leaning in. I don't understand, her mother says, pulling back. Pearl shrugs theatrically. She watches her mother begin to fidget. Gotta problem? she asks politely. Go away, Pearl, you are a bad girl, her mother shouts. But Pearl doesn't respond. Soon her mother is keening, and her father runs upstairs, pushing past Pearl with his arms outstretched. I don't like that person in my room, she mumbles into his neck. Get rid of her. Nonsense, her father says, you don't really mean that, and drags Pearl forwards. There is a series of knocks at the front door, and Pearl and her mother are alone again. Well, I s'pose this really is ta-ta, Pearl says, curtsying with an imaginary skirt. Her mother climbs unsteadily out of bed and goes to stand facing into the corner, her nightdress caught between her buttocks. When the male nurses come to lead her out, she points with a stiff arm at Pearl and states clearly, make no mistake, that one is to blame for all of this. Then she starts to fight, holding onto the doorframe. Struggling on the landing, her father looks back at Pearl. I want to know what your mother means, he says.

A special day

In her nightdress, Pearl's mother lashes out at the two men who are trying to support her down the stairs. Pearl has moved, sinuous as an eel, between the group on the landing, and now watches her mother's descent from below. She sees, in brutal flashes, her mother's maroon, tufted slit and white thighs each time she kicks, hears the smacking sounds her bare feet make as they hit the stairway walls. The group on the stairs collapses. Her mother, now prone, slips from the nurses' grip and shrieks as she slides down, landing like a sack of stones on the tiled floor. Pearl moves back, out of her mother's reach. The Blob is standing in the kitchen doorway, and Pearl bumps into him. He is trembling, so she takes hold of his hand. Be calm, she whispers. Things will be fine soon. But he begins to cry. I hate you, he shouts, struggling to get past. Mummy! he gasps, as he drops to his knees and tries to stroke his mother's small, restless feet. Mummy, don't go! Pearl grabs the back of his collar. Get up! she shouts, pulling. Leave it! But her brother shrugs her off, clumsily arranging his mother's nightdress. Everything around Pearl slowly begins to spin and melt; the red-faced men in their white coats, her father, sitting on the stairs, the wet chin and blue eyes of the woman on the floor, her distraught brother, they are bleeding into each other and revolving silently. Pearl feels herself being dragged in as they pick up speed. It's ridiculous, she thinks, spinning helplessly. None of this matters. But try as she might, she cannot get free of the mess in the hall.

Closed

Not you! You stay where you are! her father shouted at Pearl over his shoulder. The group surrounding her mother somehow got down the path and gathered around the waiting ambulance. He was holding up his wife's blonde head as if it were a precious bowl. The Blob climbed in, still crying, still managing to keep hold of his mother's nightdress. Then, after a final struggle with the jerking body, they were gone. Pearl stands alone, fixed in the open doorway, like the girl in a painting of a lonely girl in a doorway. Not one window blinks in the deserted street. The parked cars look abandoned, each garden gate guards a path, each garden hedge seems enormous. The quiet minutes tick on, but soon Pearl feels a cold breeze blowing her out of the house, down the path and on, across the field. For once, she doesn't want to leave, and manages to turn and look back. There is the half-open front door, the spotless, red porch floor, the tiles and bricks, all shrinking, pulling back fast. Or, thinks Pearl, fighting against the force of the buffeting air, am I running away? Am I getting bigger and bigger? How will I ever force myself back in? Her father's voice shouting Not you! strikes her face again and again until her mind blanks. On the breeze she recognises her brother's sobs. Suddenly, far away in the tiny house she sees the door swinging shut. Pearl knows she must get inside before it slams. She zigzags across the field, the wind ripping at the roots of her hair, and like a diver, launches herself over the gate, up the path and in through the door's final, grudging sliver of space.

Dressing up

Pearl falls deeply asleep on the bottom step and, when she wakes, thinks how wonderful the stairwell used to be. She remembers playing with her brother halfway up. The fun they had. Then she sees the worn soles of her mother's slippers face down on separate steps. The empty, scuffed walls tower around Pearl, and seem to reverberate with the sounds of slapping flesh. The house is hanging back, unsure, shutting her out, and Pearl knows she has to get busy. In the kitchen she flicks the kettle's switch. While it boils she stiffly climbs the stairs and enters her parents' room. Immediately she strips the rumpled bed. Picking up items that belong on the dressing table, she begins to sing; la–la, la–la, la–la, on and on, two notes, just the same as always. She opens the window, sitting to watch the curtains billow out and back before she remakes the bed, leaving the coverlet to lap the floor. Finally, she opens both wardrobe doors and looks at her mother's clothes. She pulls out an iridescent black dress, the full skirt bumpy with embroidered scarlet stars, and drops it over her head. It's a special dress, the perfumed collar low. Pearl sees her reflection. The dress looks like a stiff frame, or a dark cage enclosing her small body. She searches for a belt and pulls it tight. Then, slipping both feet into her mother's high-heeled, narrow mules, she gathers her gleaming hair into a pleat, winding her curl for a moment around her finger. A sound makes her turn quickly. In the gloom she sees her father silhouetted in the doorway. What do you think you're doing? he asks quietly.

But

Pearl is so happy she leaps onto her parents' bed. Everything is happening in slow motion. Her pounding feet ruck up the heavy coverlet, creating little soft mounds and ridges on its surface. With each jump her hair loosens until it flies upwards, opening like a scroll. An unstoppable, shimmering snake of words writhes from her mouth and undulates towards her father, but she can't see his face. Her eyes can only make out the glow surrounding him. You and me, Daddy! she screams. Inside her head beautiful pictures burst and fade and her heart ignites, flaring like a Catherine wheel. When she's finished telling him her plans and can't bounce any more, she floats down onto the crumpled milk-white bed cover. The silky black fabric of her mother's dress sighs as it deflates. It feels clingy and wet against her bare legs. Gradually she comes to herself and sees the wardrobe doors still standing open, the curtains billowing and there, in the doorway, her father's solid, unmoving shape. She opens her arms and beckons with her fingers. Please come and cuddle with me, she coaxes. As if electrified, her father leaps towards the bed and grabs Pearl by the shoulders. He yanks her towards him, and she finally sees his face. Get this thing off, he grunts, and rips the dress across the neck, forcing it down over her shoulders to where the belt holds it together at Pearl's waist. Her arms are pinned painfully to her sides. She is staring into her father's eyes as he drops her to the floor. Then he leaves the room and slams the door. Pearl calls to him from where she lies drumming her feet. But Daddy, she cries, don't go!

Outside

Pearl heard howling on her way to the woods. Almost, she expected to see wolves loping by her side. She'd leapt the swollen stream and watched as the trees shifted to lock her out. For the first time in her life there was not the smallest space for her to slip through. She'd listened to the slithery sound of the undergrowth tangling itself shoulder high. Deep in the woods, all the birds were mute, frozen on each lovely branch. Now Pearl is hungry and cold; her legs are glass stems. She looks at her fingers. They shoot out like crooked twigs, stretched almost to snapping point. She's asleep on top of the mountain in amongst the whinberries and harebells and beads of sheep poo, dreaming that she's lying on a mountain, in the rain. Above her, razor-sharp stars slice through the clouds. Down in the valley, a town twinkles. Through the hundreds of lighted windows she can see families gathered together. Each mother is Pearl's mother, each father is Pearl's. And there is her brother, in every house, over and over. But the fourth figure, wearing her clothes, with her colourless cowl of hair, has a face like a dirty smudge and is fading fast. Pearl runs on fragile legs from house to house, her whip-like fingers sieving air, trying to bang the doors and windows, her eyes blinded, her mouth a demented hole. But not one of the mothers or fathers or brothers looks up. They smile at each other, and warm themselves at identical, purring fires. Oh Daddy! Pearl wails. It's me, your daughter! And simultaneously, all across the town, fathers in firelit rooms get up and shut the curtains.

Acknowledgements

Many thanks to Ros Porter and everyone at Oneworld for their flexibility and flair. Thanks also to Jenny Parrott and Charlotte Van Wijk, and likewise to my brilliant, calm and supportive agent Cathryn Summerhayes.

Thanks yet again to my straight-talking, generous and all-round gorgeous writing group, Edgeworks: Ruth Smith, Andrew Smith, Norman Schwenk, Jane Blank and Claire Syder.

Also, to my friends and family, a resounding thank you.

And most of all, I am beyond grateful to my husband Norman Schwenk for his loving good sense, unswerving faith and serious braininess.